The attraction between Alyssa and Sheikh Tariq bin Hamed Al Zahini was as immediate as sunstroke, bearing with it all the heat of the desert. But Alyssa had a job to do, and Tariq was promised to his young cousin. So whatever she felt for him could not be allowed to grow . . .

SUNSTROKE

BY

ELIZABETH OLDFIELD

MILLS & BOON LIMITED
15–16 BROOK'S MEWS
LONDON W1A 1DR

First published in Great Britain 1985
by Mills & Boon Limited

© Elizabeth Oldfield 1985

Australian copyright 1985
Philippine copyright 1986
This edition 1986

ISBN 0 263 75282 8

Set in Monophoto Plantin 11 on 12 pt.
01-0286 – 44798

Made and printed in Great Britain by
Richard Clay (The Chaucer Press) Ltd,
Bungay, Suffolk

CHAPTER ONE

RAS-AL-KHAN baked beneath a white-hot sun. Afternoon in high summer, and the heat which scorched like a blast from an open furnace had reduced outdoor life to a virtual standstill. The city was an inert building-block tumble of concrete, colour-sapped by the glare. From her vantage point at the windows of the penthouse suite, Alyssa searched among the bleached landscape for signs of activity. A trickle of cars moved on the dual carriageway far below. There was a lone juggernaut, windscreen glittering like diamonds, which swung on to the sand verge and stopped with a jerk. A trio of matchstick figures spilled from the cab and she grinned as they hurdled the mid-road crash barrier, robes hoisted to knee-level, and rushed with comic haste for the shade of a palm. The trio was in the minority; anyone with any sense was indoors, preferring the cool comfort of the air-conditioner to the merciless *sauté* of that molten ball high in the sky.

'As the latest recruit, what's your opinion of our illustrious radio station?' asked the florid-faced man beside her.

Startled, Alyssa came back to life. Daydreaming was out with the rules, she was expected to contribute her share of conversation to the lunchtime drinks party.

'I'm enjoying working at Radio Ras-Al-Khan

very much,' she replied automatically, and treated her fellow guest to a vivid smile.

He had said he was a banker, but she had forgotten his name. He would not have forgotten hers, she was certain, for in the five minutes since they'd been introduced he had taken her, step by step, through an intense verbal questionnaire. Name? Alyssa Brett. Marital Status? Widow. Residence? The Colonnade, this very apartment block, though in one-bedroom accommodation down on the sixth floor. Date of arrival in the Arabian Gulf? Roughly a month ago. Purpose? To become the third, and sole female, member of the radio band's trio of presenters.

The banker was on the brink of a follow-up remark when his wife appeared to claim his attention, leaving Alyssa free to return to the view which attracted her like a magnet. Each time she gazed down on the city's geometric sprawl something different caught her eye. Squat flat-roofed buildings, sprouting television antennae like stick insects, spread for miles; and among them she could pick out graceful minarets, the golden dazzle of domes, tamarisk trees in dark green splodges. Her eyes lifted. Today the airport runways were visible and, in the far distance, a pearly haze indicated where the city disappeared into desert.

Switching her stance, she followed the curve of the Corniche, a sophisticated coastal promenade, lush with oleander and jasmine, which was believed to owe its inspiration to the sea road linking Nice with Monte Carlo. And against the Corniche lapped the turquoise waters of the Gulf, where a parade of oil tankers moved like ponderous elephants towards a gauzy horizon. So much oil, so much wealth. She sighed, sucked back into her obsession—totting up the finances with which it was vital she work a miracle.

Damned money! Alyssa deplored the hold it had over her life. Each night she fell asleep nagged by worry, and awoke still brooding. There was no escape. The sheikhdom of Ras-Al-Khan dripped affluence, as if determined to thumb its nose at her plight. Polished limousines purred through the streets, private jets taxied around the airport, and clogging the suburbs were showplace mansions where architects had been handed *carte blanche*. Even the municipal buildings, irreverently nicknamed 'Suroor's follies', resembled lavish fairytale castles, and her mouth twitched in amusement as she focused on the spun-sugar turrets of the Electricity Board's offices below. The inspiration there had been pure Walt Disney!

She swivelled, wondering if she should retrace her steps to Brough Maury, her escort. Standing on tiptoe, Alyssa peered to find him, tall and fair-haired, happily involved in conversation with a clutch of admiring females. She decided not to interrupt and instead took note of her immediate surroundings. Accommodation was provided as part of the package deal in working for Ras-Al-Khan's Ministry of Information and Culture, and what accommodation! Her own apartment resembled a picture-spread from a glossy magazine— off-white carpets and Swedish furniture—but Norman Harding, her host and head of the country's broadcasting service, lived in breath-taking style. A seventeenth-century Chinese jet screen filled one corner of the vast lounge and now Alyssa's gaze travelled to the brass-studded chests, the Bokhara rugs, the settees upholstered in soft yellow leather which lined the sunken seating area.

And the plants! How she would love to fill her apartment with the spring-green ferns which cascaded from copper buckets and the creamy plumes of the Night Queen shrubs. Maybe the antiques would be forever beyond her purse, but she could have splashed out on pot plants if only ... *If only*. How many times since Douglas's death had she repeated those two little words?

Her lips clamped together. More than intended had seeped from her first month's salary, but still she had saved enough to send a healthy payment to her creditor, Nigel Dutton. A payment routed through her sister, Meg, in order that her whereabouts be kept a secret. This month her expenses would be cut to the bone. She would live on air if needs be. Paying off the debt at speed was the only hope she had. A slender hope. For a moment Alyssa cringed. If only she was not at Nigel Dutton's mercy—at the mercy of a fat slimy predator. If only ...

'About the radio,' the banker began again, as his wife scampered off to speak to an old friend. 'A smart girl like you must have realised that——' A hiatus in the general hum of conversation abruptly made him alter course. 'My word, old Norm's hit the jackpot this time,' he murmured.

On the far side of the room their host was

pumping hands, welcoming in a party of four Arabs in flowing white robes. Alyssa noticed how, all around her, neckties were being adjusted, hair styles patted, how everyone was standing a little straighter as if they hoped to catch the attention of these new arrivals. Even Brough had paused in his soliloquy.

'Who are they?' she whispered, as the buzz of voices resumed.

The banker leant closer. 'The bearded chap Norman's fawning over is none other than His Excellency Sheikh Karim bin Hamed Al Zahini, grandson of the ruler, Sheikh Ahmad,' he told her. 'Karim's second in line to the sheikhdom, after his uncle, Suroor.'

'And he's also Minister of Information and Culture,' Alyssa exclaimed with relish, pleased to have at last seen the sheikh who was, on paper, also her boss.

'Yes, among other things. His Excellency's being groomed for his eventual role as ruler of Ras-Al-Khan, so he's involved in a wide span of interests. He's titular head of the Information Ministry, but other matters intrude. Karim has no option but to leave the nitty-gritty to a wad of underlings—like our host,' her companion added, not bothering to hide a sneer.

'Sheikh Karim isn't in a position to get to grips?' she confirmed, realising how that could explain a lot.

'No, though to be fair he does his best. I understand he's reorganised the Arabic output on both radio and TV, but so far the English programmes have been left to the inadequacies of

old Norm,' the banker said, flinging a disdainful
look at their still ingratiating host.

'Do you think we'll be introduced to the
sheikh?' Alyssa enquired, unwilling to become
involved in a discussion of their host's short-
comings. Not that such discussions were unusual,
indeed gossip appeared to be the glue which held
certain strata of the expatriate community
together. A shiver ran down her spine. What a
field day everyone would have if *her* inadequacies
ever leaked out!

The banker shook his head. 'You and I are too
low down the social scale to be worthy of an
audience. In any case, Karim won't stay longer
than five minutes. I'm surprised he's here at all,
but I expect old Norm's been angling for a visit
for months and His Excellency has given in and
agreed to appear as a token gesture. He'll be in
and out, mark my words. Making small talk isn't
Karim's scene.'

At this point the banker's wife returned,
jealously placing a hand on his arm, so he rolled
his eyes and transferred his allegiance. Alyssa
didn't mind. She was fascinated by Sheikh Karim
and his colleagues. In four weeks in the Gulf she
had had sparse contact with the locals, and was
beginning to wonder if her chances of gaining
access to their world might be slim. The women
in their black silk robes, faces covered by veils or
beak-like masks, were shy, and the men ...
Limpid dark eyes often rested on her, doubtless
attracted by her blonde tresses, yet those looks
had been swift and guilty.

The Arab party had split. Sheikh Karim and

two sidekicks were meeting some of the most prestigious guests, while the fourth man had been claimed by the twittery Mrs Harding. He was taller than the others, his shoulders broad beneath the snow-white *dishdasha*, and something in his confident stance drew Alyssa's attention. Head bent to catch his hostess's words, his face was hidden by the fall of his headdress, but there was no doubt he was someone special. She longed to know his identity, but the banker and his wife had begun to bicker and she could not interrupt.

Alyssa was watching the tall Arab when, without warning, he raised his head and as if guided by radar, his gaze circled the room to stop on her. Her heartbeat faltered. The dark eyes which had caught hers were not guilty, neither was his look swift. He had straightened to give a cool and direct appraisal, one arched brow lifting ever so slightly as if her consternation amused him. The vivid intelligence which shone from his long-lashed eyes warned that here was a forceful personality. Proud and strong, he looked like the kind of man who cut a clear path to his objective, someone who knew what he wanted from life. His sheer physical presence was making her skin prickle. Alyssa's cheeks began to burn. Wiser to lower her gaze, but how? Her eyes were coupled to his. She was trapped, caught in the stranger's power.

The Arab appeared to be around thirty, sultry of skin and darkly moustached, though not as swarthy nor as hawk-nosed as his companions. Glamorous in the alien robes, his clear-cut features demonstrated a desert heritage. The white *kaffia* covered his hair, but Alyssa could see that his brow was broad and the determined jaw was as if fine cut from granite. She plucked awkwardly at the drifting ends of the silk scarf which fell to her shoulder, wanting to look away and yet not wanting to. An invisible chain had been roped around her. The stranger was intent on dragging her into his orbit, although they remained yards apart. His self-assurance was impressive for, despite this intimate eye contact, he was calmly continuing the conversation with his hostess. How could he remain so detached when he was transmitting such heart-stopping messages?

'You're looking very elegant,' a light voice said into her ear and the spell snapped. Alyssa spun round, grateful to be released, the blood surging through her veins as though she had hit the tape at the finish of a five-mile sprint. Lennie Leith, who worked with her and Brough on the radio team, had arrived. A part-owner of a local boutique, the young man was fanatical about fashion, and now he assessed her lemon two-piece suit. 'Like the cropped jacket. And the colour suits you.'

'Thanks. Who's that man over there?' Why did her voice sound so high and trembly?

'Which one?' asked Lennie, flipping a hank of pony-brown hair from his brow. He paused to whistle up a waiter and order himself a drink, and then it was too late. The banker's five-minute span had been accurate, for in a flurry of farewells the VIPs disappeared.

'The tall one.' Alyssa's reply was crisp with irritation. The young man had dawdled over an answer when she had *needed* to know.

He shrugged. 'Maybe a friend of Karim's, or an *aide-de-camp*, or his driver.'

'His driver?' she asked, surprised.

'Could be. Arabs aren't as stuffy about protocol as us, they're far more democratic. The highest in the land will befriend the lowest. They're all on first name terms.'

'But a driver at a drinks party? I thought——'

A burst of laughter released her tension, and Alyssa began to scold herself. Eyes across a crowded room was banal. Her reaction had been foolish. What had happened to the cool rationale she had learned to use with the opposite sex? Maybe a touch of sunstroke or the unfamiliar setting of a foreign country had reduced her guard. Within a fortnight of Douglas's death she had discovered how a young widow is considered fair game, and had no intention of being peppered with gun shot. Now most men were frozen out on sight. Even true blue characters, like Brough, were treated to a brisk friendship which rejected any admission they might be male, and she female. What stupid quirk had made her feel like spending the rest of the afternoon simply gazing into those dark eyes?

'I must learn to separate the wheat from the chaff,' she joked. 'Here's me, living in hope of an Arabian prince waylaying me in the supermarket and offering mind-blowing sums for my favours——'

'Me, too,' Lennie interrupted shamelessly.

'——but if I confuse princes with the man who drives the car!' Alyssa giggled, easier now. Her response to the tall Arab must have been the result of one too many pre-luncheon drinks.

'I doubt there'll be any more Middle Eastern princes putting in an appearance today, sweetie,' Lennie said, adjusting the cuff of his pink satin shirt. 'And Karim's out of reach. He's been happily married to a lady called Noora for the past ten years, and is reputed to be the very essence of the family man.' Her colleague peered across the room, making a census of the assembled party. 'I see the adoring Brough has deserted you.'

'Actually I deserted him, and he isn't adoring.'

'No?' Lennie obviously thought otherwise, for he nudged her in the ribs and leered, 'Hasn't he revealed how much he lusts after your beautiful body?'

Alyssa sighed. 'We're just friends,' she insisted.

'I wouldn't be too sure. Your days could well be numbered,' he said darkly, glancing again at Brough and the surrounding females. 'What d'you bet he's droning on about that play he's written? The thing's bound to be dismal "anyone for tennis" stuff.'

'Nonsense! It's a comedy and sounds hilarious. I'm looking forward to tackling the manuscript.'

Lennie affected acute astonishment. 'You don't intend to type out that mountain of scribbles he's been toting around in his briefcase for months?'

'I most certainly do. Brough is commandeering a typewriter from the general office and bringing it over to my apartment. The play will be typed in my spare time.'

'A labour of love?' he asked slyly.

Alyssa shook her head. 'Brough insisted I take payment.'

'Aha! Saw a way of coining in the extra *dirham*, did you?' Lennie jibed, exhibiting characteristic cat claws and a little too much perspicacity.

'No, I did not!' she protested, but was unable to stop a hasty analysis of her motives. Time hung heavy—due to a sparse workload at the radio station—yet had she offered to type Brough's play subconsciously expecting payment? Had it been a selfish money-making gesture and not just one of friendship? Was she becoming so obsessed with the need for cash that her greedy little hands were grab-grab-grabbing without any help from her? Oh heavens, she hoped not. She lined up further denials, but Lennie had turned away, luckily losing interest. Alyssa had few illusions. The young man liked her, as much as he was capable of liking anyone, but he'd sacrifice her reputation without a qualm if there was a chance for him to bask in the limelight as he delivered a delicious muck-raking tale. And what a tale he'd be able to narrate if he ever discovered why acquiring cash was so important to her!

'Roll on September when the temperature cools down,' he commented, scowling out at the sunshine. 'One hundred and eleven in the shade is a killer. Those who can escape to more equable climes have. This place is dead socially in the summer. Last night I was strutting my stuff before a fun-packed audience of seventeen, and that included a cat and two cockroaches.'

'Don't you ever feel guilty about accepting a

fully-fledged salary from Ras-Al-Khan's government when you devote so much of your time to the discos?' she asked, for in addition to radio work and his interest in the boutique, Lennie also acted as link man at a couple of hotel discotheques.

He hooted with scornful laughter. 'Never!'

'Well, you should.' Alyssa could not conceal her contempt. 'What goes on here amazes me. Everyone contributes the very minimum they can to the radio and——'

'Your only motivation in working for Radio Ras-Al-Khan is the money,' he cut in, not wishing to be reminded of any deficiencies. 'You're no different to the rest of us.'

'Yes, I am! I've tried to persuade Mr Harding to let me produce something worthwhile instead of the damn Top Twenty being broadcast *ad nauseam*. Grief! Record shows fill the bulk of transmission. I've yet to hear a single stimulating interview or discussion.'

Lennie treated her protest to deaf ears. 'Remember you mentioned you'd like to do some modelling to earn a bit of pin-money?' he asked.

'Did I?' Alyssa blinked. She cared about her radio work, cared deeply, and found it hard to switch lanes while half her mind continued to bewail the laxness of the station and its employees.

'Ages ago. You said you'd modelled a little back home, and I said I had a Filipino photographer friend called Byron, and you said to mention your name.' Lennie paused, relieved to see he had diverted her. 'Well, Byron has a big photo assignment brewing. A major hotel's opening a sportswear outlet in their shopping arcade and a swanky brochure's planned. Byron needs a stylish blonde with bags of sex appeal simmering below the surface.'

She laughed. 'And that's me?'

'You must realise every heterosexual male here today is itching to get you into bed?' he jeered. 'Even I can see you're a hot-blooded creature. On the surface you're a peaches and cream girl, but ...' He waited, like an actor building maximum effect. 'But that lower lip is a shade too full, a dead cert for sensuality.'

'Shut up, Lennie,' she warned, in a low fierce voice.

He heard the bite of anger. 'The modelling shouldn't take up too much time, just a few hours one morning,' he said, changing the subject. 'The pay's terrific, and if this first job goes well perhaps Byron'll use you for some other stuff? Why not ring him? He'd like you to visit his studio, so he can check I didn't lie when I raved about you, and I expect you'll need to report to the store when the various outfits are chosen.' He moved a hand. 'I dare say there could be a fitting or two.'

Alyssa hesitated. A few hours one morning was lengthening into a series of appointments, and a jumble of difficulties thumped around inside her head. Her first commitment was to Radio Ras-Al-Khan, could the modelling be fitted around her schedule at the station? Was taking on second-string work unethical? Not strictly speaking, and she was under-employed. Lennie drew cash from his boutique and Brough spent hours writing plays in the hope of striking it rich, why shouldn't she fill her off-duty hours profitably?

'I'll 'phone Byron this evening,' Alyssa decided.

She knew there was no hope of reaching Nigel Dutton's deadline, but the more money she had at her disposal, the stronger her bargaining position. Her stomach plunged. *If* he was prepared to bargain.

CHAPTER TWO

ALYSSA'S impatient gaze scoured over the two men who sat so disconsolately in the presenters' lounge.

'I don't know why you both seem so surprised. A shake-up was long overdue.'

'Whose side are you on?' Lennie demanded peevishly.

'The side of sparkier programmes,' she retaliated. 'The English-speaking proportion of Ras-Al-Khan's population has suffered long enough. It's about time they had something decent to listen to. And, quite frankly, the prospect of an individual who cares taking control makes me want to jump for joy. You must admit Mr Harding's monumentally incapable of providing a lead.'

'What makes you imagine this Sheikh Tariq is such good news, when you don't know a blind thing about him?' Lennie enquired.

'Whoever he is,' Brough intervened, 'he's obviously given old Norm a rare horsewhipping. I've never seen him so subdued, nor heard such a long-winded prevarication. Though I suppose defending yourself, without appearing to do so, must have been tricky.'

It was a week since the drinks party, and an hour since Mr Harding had gathered the radio personnel together and dropped his bombshell—

or Sheikh Tariq's bombshell to be exact. Voice struggling out from a raw larynx, Norman Harding had explained that the *dolce vita* they had taken for granted was over. Programmes were to be overhauled, broadcasting hours extended, striking economies made, new rules drawn up.

'The screws are being turned, *hard*,' he had warned, and added in a moment of pique and indiscretion, 'The sheikh says he sees no reason why the state should subsidise a gang of freeloaders.'

'Freeloaders!' Brough had spluttered, amongst other rumblings of protest.

And now the three presenters were working through the implications of being regarded as underworked and overpaid.

'How do I continue my night club activities if I'm expected to be pinned to the blasted microphone until all hours?' demanded Lennie, smiting a dramatic fist against his brow.

'Looks like you'll have to say goodbye to being the big disco king,' Brough replied, unable to resist a smile at the thought of his colleague being chopped down to size.

'So gloat!' came the sneer. 'But you realise what this guy is? He's a hatchet man. So he's only to be with us for six damned weeks, but six weeks is long enough for him to chop out anything and anyone he considers dead wood, and then march off leaving bloody chaos behind him.'

For the first time Alyssa's enthusiasm for the unknown sheikh wavered. Her contract was for eighteen months, but she had banked on staying three years. She needed three years. How could she accumulate the necessary cash to rid herself of Nigel Dutton in less? It was impossible. If she was honest, the cheque she had sent to him last month would have altered nothing. Dry-mouthed all of a sudden, she imagined the agony of having Douglas's exploits dissected in open court. That must never happen. She would move mountains to ensure her husband could rest in peace.

'I know a bit about Sheikh Tariq,' Brough offered unexpectedly. 'Last week I was at an oilman's party when Karim's younger brother, Tariq, was mentioned. This has to be the same guy. I'd say we shouldn't underestimate him. He's involved in handling Ras-Al-Khan's share of the oil market and he's a shrewd operator. He's fixed some pretty lucrative deals. The Ruler, his grandfather, thinks very highly of him and so, I gathered, do the oil fraternity.'

Lennie patted away a yawn. 'Does he have a harem?'

'He's not a playboy,' Brough said, throwing the disc jockey an impatient glance. 'I understand he's poised to marry one of Sheikh Suroor's daughters.'

'So where's this lover been hiding?' asked Lennie, adopting a Mae West voice. 'I've never heard of him before.'

'Apparently he was based in London until a couple of months ago, though he commuted to New York on a regular basis.' Brough scratched his chin. 'I think they said he has a degree in petroleum engineering, plus an MBA from Harvard. He came top in his year.'

'But why would an oil expert cast an eye over the media?' Alyssa frowned.

'No idea. Old Norm reckons the sheikh's looking for fresh ideas on day-to-day content. I wonder if he'd be interested in drama?'

Lennie gave a hoot of laughter. 'You're not imagining there's a chance of getting that play of yours aired?'

'And why not?' demanded Brough, defending his territory.

'Stop fighting,' Alyssa pleaded. 'This is the time for closing ranks, not picking petty quarrels. Let's decide what we want to say to the sheikh when we meet him in the boardroom in . . .' she looked at her watch, '. . . two hours' time.'

Of course, they didn't close ranks nor decide what they wanted to say. Lennie had indulged in some falsetto posturing, claiming the sheikh was a new broom who would rapidly lose interest, and Brough had decided there was sufficient time before the meeting for him to grab a swim. They both disappeared, leaving Alyssa alone in the small lounge which also served as office, waiting room and bolt hole. She took stock. Impressing this new overlord was vital because, although he may be temporary, he could have a say in the future—*her* future. She needed to show him how bright and capable she was, then he would be willing to pay for her services over the three-year span she so vitally required.

Alyssa was a professional. Back home she had been an innovative and hard-working member of the local radio station's staff, and had refused several offers from a London airwave. London! She grew wistful. Jerry Thompson had almost gone down on his knees to beg her to join his team and, after Douglas's death, she had been all set to agree. But days before signing Jerry's contract, a chance look at a newspaper had revealed Ras-Al-Khan's requirement of a newscaster, quoting a vastly inflated salary. Alyssa knew what had had to be done. So—goodbye, London.

What were her chances of charming this unknown sheikh? she wondered, as she brushed her hair and re-knotted the black silk scarf around the snake of shiny ash-blonde hair which fell across one shoulder. Today she was wearing a silk two-piece in stark black and white stripes, a soft belt clinching her waist. The unrelenting colours emphasised her fair femininity, but so what? She would receive one of those swift and guilty glances, and be steadfastly ignored. Just because he had lived in the West he wouldn't necessarily accept the concept of the career woman. The Arabic way was to sequester females at home. And if, as Brough had reported, he was so much the businessman, he would be too engrossed in planning programmes and cutting costs to notice her. The image of an oil sheikh cutting costs brought a bubble of wry amusement. What she would give to swap his financial problems for hers!

Two hours later, armed with a list of programme improvements she intended to suggest, Alyssa made her way upstairs to the boardroom. The wide landing was empty. What had happened to Brough and Lennie? She checked her watch to confirm it was bare minutes to kick-off. Didn't they realise being punctual was important? She went over to the windows, but only a gardener could be seen down below in the courtyard, watering the purple and white bougainvillaea.

Behind her sounded the click of footsteps. Someone was striding up the stairs, two at a time.

'Where on earth have you been?' Alyssa demanded, spinning to administer a jokey reprimand. Her heart missed a beat, before starting up again on an uneven tempo. Instead of her colleagues, she had been joined by a tall figure clad in the white robes of the desert. 'I'm sorry, I didn't expect——' she blustered, fingering a wisp of hair from her cheek. Her voice faded. The man was the Arab who had given her such a penetrating appraisal at Norman Harding's party—the driver. Her gaze bounced from him. Once was enough. She would not be so foolish as to allow those fine dark eyes to bedazzle her a second time. 'Are you looking for your boss?' Alyssa asked, and a thick black brow lifted in query. 'Boss, master,' she pronounced, reaching the decision that he would not speak much English. Once she had done six weeks' television for schools, and now she used the same deliberately clear tones. 'Your master is Sheikh Karim, you understand?' How could she avoid those lynx-like eyes with their heavy fringe of curling lashes? Eyes which found amusement in her efforts to get her message across. Alyssa had a horrible feeling he knew precisely the affect he was having on her composure. 'Sheikh Karim not here,' she flustered in pidgin English. She pointed towards the boardroom door. 'His brother, Sheikh Tariq, is holding a meeting in there in a few minutes' time. You know Sheikh Tariq, little brother?' She distanced about two inches between her thumb and forefinger. 'Tariq, little brother,' she repeated.

He gave a lazy, taunting smile. 'I can assure you I'm not that little. You do me a disservice, Mrs Brett.'

An impudent gleam in his eyes made her wonder if he had picked up some totally different interpretation. Her cheeks flamed. This man was never a driver. He was too self-assured, too well-spoken, too—— She saw that his robes were of the finest quality, that the cufflinks at his wrists were embossed gold. He carried a bundle of blue plastic files under one arm.

'You're Sheikh Tariq!'

Alyssa hated being so slow on the uptake, but reasoned thought was proving difficult beneath the gaze of this sultry corsair. Too late, she wondered if she was supposed to address him as 'Your Excellency' or 'Sir'.

'I am.' He strode into the boardroom, leaving her to follow. 'I've been attempting to prod the general office into action. The secretaries down there don't seem capable of coping with two jobs at once, let alone three.' He pitched his armful of files on to the table and turned. 'I'm pleased to meet you—again.' His handclasp was firm. 'Now, let's get down to business. I've been listening to the demo tape you submitted before you joined us, Mrs Brett, and it's excellent.'

Seating himself at the head of the table, he began rapidly sorting through the files. His industry surprised her. On the rare occasions she had met with locals, she had been drenched in Arabic hyperbole and flowery diplomacy, so this cut-and-thrust attitude came as a shock.

'My demo tape?' Alyssa felt very much as if she was swimming underwater. The tape consisted of snippets of previous work she had done, linked with music. Mr Harding had never referred to it after her interview, though at the time he had listened with great interest.

The sheikh looked up, surprised to discover she was still standing. 'Do be seated. The human interest portions are particularly good. Why haven't you done similar work here?'

Having first been fascinated by his eyes, Alyssa now discovered his voice was fascinating, too. He sounded as if he gargled daily with molasses, for he had a low rich drawl, smudged and smoky with the patterns of the Arabic tongue. His English, however, was immaculate. Couldn't she detect a trace of some regional English accent? No, she must be mistaken.

'The opportunity hasn't arisen so far,' Alyssa explained, sitting on the chair he had indicated.

'You don't wait for opportunities to arise, you make them.'

'But I'm not in a position to tell——' she began, knocked askew by this unexpected censure.

'Don't bother with excuses.'

Crushed, she looked at him. Was this blade-edged tycoon the man who had smiled so teasingly only moments ago? Alyssa sat up a little straighter, determined to defend herself. She deserved a fair hearing.

'I don't make the policy decisions around here, and——'

'And it's easier to lie in the sun than do an honest day's work for an honest day's pay?' he thrust. He was a master with the rapier.

'No!'

'Then you're unique. I understand the Colonnade's pool deck is constantly blessed with at least one member of the radio team, which equals the state of affairs at the studio. One here, one there. It's bewildering to imagine what the third member gets up to.'

Alyssa would have bet her life on Sheikh Tariq never being plagued by bewilderment. Right now he was playing Russian roulette to his own rules, six out of six words being loaded. Her eyes skimmed his aristocratic stature, the white headdress held in place by the circular black ropes of the *agal*, his fine *dishdasha*. The glint of the cutlass in his look convinced her his ancestors had kidnapped frail damsels and tormented them for their pleasure.

'I'd welcome the opportunity to organise some programmes with local interest,' she began. 'And——'

'What kind of local interest?'

'Maybe if you'd allow me to finish at least one sentence I'd be able to tell you,' she snapped, so full of righteous indignation that she forgot about being subservient.

Dark brows rose in surprise. 'Go ahead.'

'I'd like to investigate the culture and heritage of the Gulf in general, and Ras-Al-Khan in particular. This metropolis was little more than a fishing village forty years ago, and there must be news stories galore in the transition. The human angle goes down well and I'll have plenty of scope for that. I could interview local people and expatriates. Surprisingly all Westerners don't spend their lives slathered in suncream,' Alyssa added, unable to resist an offensive. 'Some are busy and vital and alert.'

The brows rose again. 'Like you?'

'Like me,' she asserted.

'Plan a trial programme and we'll discuss it tomorrow.' He pushed back his cuff to inspect a heavy gold watch. 'Where are your partners in crime? They appear to be late.' Protesting that they were only four minutes late seemed to be pointless, and she was thankful when he didn't pursue the matter. Instead he smiled and said, 'I'm sure you're wondering how I come to be here?'

'Well . . . yes,' Alyssa admitted.

'I tend to wonder myself.' Amusement flickered in his dark eyes. 'To be brief, my brother, Karim, has relinquished his role as Information Minister to concentrate on Defence, and I've been brought in to tie up the ends he didn't get around to.'

'You're to be the new Minister?'

He shook his head. 'There are other plans for me.' She never learned what the plans were, for at that moment a knock came on the door. 'Enter,' he commanded, and Brough and Lennie came in. The sheikh greeted their apologies with barbed civility and began the meeting. All the facts were at his fingertips, and after defining areas he had marked down for reorganisation, he began firing off rebukes, one by one. 'Several of the ground rules appear to have been overlooked. For a start, everyone works the hours stipulated in their contracts and when I say work, I mean you are to be physically present at the studio.'

'What if there's nothing to do?' queried Lennie, exhibiting a desire to walk the greasy pole. 'We normally check out if we're not needed at the microphone.'

Alyssa wished she could curl up into a ball and roll away. How could Lennie be so crass as to imagine such admissions would be condoned? She slid a sideways look to the head of the table, and when she discovered the lynx eyes resting on her, a shockwave rippled. That slumbrous gaze was too critical.

'There'll be far more work once the air time's increased,' she pointed out, needing to make amends and show she was not tarred with the same brush.

'That's true, Mrs Brett,' the sheikh agreed. 'But a three-strong team is extravagant when you consider the amount of wallpaper music and imported trash which goes out at present. A trained chimpanzee could handle the entire workload, standing on his head.' Lennie laughed at this, but he laughed alone. Brough and Alyssa were well aware jokes were not being marketed. 'I consider two announcers are feasible, just.'

'Two?' she echoed, as terror stabbed. She was

the last one in, did that mean she would be the first one out? Did the fact that she was a woman count against her? Maybe you only had to scratch Sheikh Tariq to discover a desert chieftain who preferred his females to be held in seclusion, out of harm's way where they could spend their days pandering to his needs and raising his children?

'Don't you agree two announcers would be ample?' he demanded.

Alyssa had to be honest. 'At present, yes. But if we replaced the imported programmes with live shows, maybe experimented with outside broadcasts? If we covered sports, produced a round-up of what's happening about town?'

'If?' He poised the word like a guillotine. 'If all that happened than I agree three presenters, or maybe more, could be usefully employed. At the moment only two are necessary.'

'Which two?'

A fierce appeal lay beneath the surface. She needed to know. Images of Nigel Dutton somersaulted through her head.

'Mrs Brett, in the Gulf we have a saying—the one who does not know the falcon will broil it. But you may be certain you're in no danger of being broiled unless I decide broiling is the fate you deserve.' His gaze left her to travel across the men. 'For now I'll settle for the status quo as far as personnel is concerned. If, as Mrs Brett has suggested, there's an inflow of energy and attitudes are sharpened, there will be no need for redundancies.' His eyes fixed on Lennie. 'And, incidentally, that inflow of energy should leave you too drained for . . . moonlighting. I trust I can rely on your co-operation? If not . . .' The muscled shoulders moved beneath his robes like those of an Arabian leopard about to spring, and now his attention was distributed between the three of them. 'If not, I'm certain Ras-Al-Khan's radio station is capable of surviving without you.'

Yes, Alyssa thought, when the meeting broke up and they all went their separate ways, Ras-Al-Khan's radio station could survive without her, but could she survive without it? Hopes of finding another job which paid so well were remote to the point of impossibility, and if a substantial portion of her debt was not cleared promptly she had no idea how she would escape Nigel Dutton's domination. Cold with fear, she mulled over her problems. If only there was a way of making money faster, faster, *faster*.

An airmail letter from Meg was waiting when she returned to her apartment that evening, and her eyes flew over the pages. Nigel Dutton had stopped Meg on the High Street and put her through the third degree!

'Can't I explain you've gone abroad? I'm sure he suspects something and I hate telling lies.'

Reading the words in her sister's neat script had Alyssa's heart hammering against her breastbone. He couldn't already be on the verge of discovering she hadn't taken the London job? She had hoped the truth could be kept from him for six months at least, but recognised that as wishful thinking. Nigel Dutton would not wait too long. All he was doing was choosing the most propitious moment, possibly when his wife departed on her annual jaunt to her cousin's home in Scotland, and then . . .

Douglas had been responsible for this middle-aged predator entering her life, although she had known of him before. As managing director of Dutton & Company, a prosperous firm of coach builders, Nigel basked in the role of leading citizen in her home town. Basked was an apt word. She could remember him as a pompous mayor, distributing prizes at school speech days, and now no civic committee was complete without his puffed-up attendance. He was at each golf club soirée, and added his substantial weight to the hierarchy of the Masonic Lodge.

Her husband's initial connection with this little tin god had been strictly business. Shortly before their marriage Douglas had bought over a small private bus company. Secondhand vehicles had been included in the purchase price but, imagining himself as the owner of a de luxe transport fleet, he soon stated these would not do.

'Wait before you order new buses, Doug. Allow the passenger volume a chance to increase,' Alyssa had implored. 'Wait until next year. Maybe there'll be more money available then.'

'Next year!' he had spat. 'I have no intention of waiting until next year.'

His face had taken on that familiarly stubborn slant and, fearful of a temper tantrum erupting, Alyssa had allowed the argument to lapse. He had had his way. Orders were placed with Dutton & Company, and in due course two brand-new buses arrived. The next thing that happened was that Mr and Mrs Dutton were invited to her home for dinner.

'You don't mind, do you?' Doug had asked, giving her that lop-sided smile of entreaty which both beguiled and warned that something might be wrong. 'Nigel's dying to meet you. He's a fan. He says he always listens to your programmes.'

Alyssa had pulled a face. 'Well, I'm not dying to meet him. He's an obnoxious character. He cheats on his wife. Everyone in town knows he goes after anything in skirts.'

'Be nice to him, Lyss.'

Something *was* wrong. Her husband preferred to keep her to himself. He was jealous if she so much as smiled at another man.

'Why?'

'He could help us,' Douglas had said, refusing to meet her eyes.

'How? You haven't fallen behind in the repayments for those damn buses, have you?' She saw his face. 'You have!'

'Just a couple of months, but Nigel's being very understanding.'

'I bet.'

'He is, Lyss. So be nice to him for me.'

For me! For Douglas's sake she had smiled when Nigel Dutton's fleshy hand had held hers a little too long, smiled when his small black eyes had removed every single thread of her clothing, smiled when Mrs Dutton, a pale mousy woman, had talked on and on about the antics of her two Chihuahuas. A fortnight later she had smiled when she and Douglas had dined at the Duttons' mock-Tudor house, five miles out of town.

Alyssa had smiled when Nigel Dutton's arm had
encircled her shoulder, his hand so casually
brushing against the side of her breast. Being in
his company reminded her of being in the
company of a crocodile, who grinned as he
weighed up the pros and cons of snapping you off
at the waist. To her horror, the evenings out
extended into a regular occurrence.

'You are keeping up the monthly payments,
Doug?' she had fretted.

'*Yes.*'

'So why must we have them round here again?
Mrs Dutton's a deadly bore, poor soul, and he's,
he's——' Alyssa had fought shy of giving chapter
and verse to the way Nigel Dutton touched her
accidentally on purpose, the way he made her
skin crawl.

'Nigel thinks you're beautiful,' Douglas had
told her. 'He reckons if he'd been twenty years
younger I'd never have stood a chance with you.'

'That's what he thinks! He's a nasty, evil-
minded man. Let's not see him anymore,' she had
pleaded.

'But Nigel knows everybody in town. He has
all the right connections. He can steer business
my way, *our* way.'

'I don't care. I just know he's dangerous.'
Douglas's eyes had skated from hers. 'You're
positive you've paid back the money you owed?'

'Stop nagging,' he had retorted, swift to take
offence. 'Can't you trust me?'

No, I can't, Alyssa had thought miserably, but
as on so many other occasions, she had backed
down. The dinner dates had continued.

Admittedly Nigel Dutton never once crossed that tacit boundary between what was acceptable and what deserved a slap on the face, but a sense of imminent doom filled her. He seemed to be biding his time, waiting, waiting. A fortnight after her husband's funeral, she had discovered what he was waiting for.

Alyssa pushed her sister's letter back into the envelope and told herself to keep a sense of proportion. But how? She owed Nigel Dutton nearly twenty thousand pounds! Yet the twenty thousand was the lesser part of the original debt. Thirty thousand had already been paid off as a result of selling her home and furniture and, if she had successfuly raised more than half, couldn't she manage the rest? Worriedly she rubbed at her brow. Was she being a coward in letting matters lie dormant for as long as possible? How she wished she had confided in Meg and Cliff, her brother-in-law, but stubborn pride and the distorted necessity of cherishing all she had left of Douglas had got in the way. Douglas! Her eyes filled with tears as she thought of her impetuous husband—the damaged boy.

CHAPTER THREE

ALYSSA donned the headphones, checked her voice level with the technician, and waited to acknowledge his start-up gesture through the glass. The familiar strains of Ras-Al-Khan's national anthem filled her ears.

'Good morning. This is Alyssa Brett welcoming you to Radio Ras-Al-Khan.' She continued with the wave length, the date and a time check. 'As usual we open our service with readings from the Holy Koran.'

Half an hour later, the news read and Brough filling the airwaves with a morning record round-up, she took herself off to the lounge. Here she would stay until an update of news and weather was broadcast at nine. Collecting a cup of coffee, Alyssa sat down and spread her papers over the desk. Sheikh Tariq had said to plan a trial programme, but she had done better. Two programmes had been planned in detail and notes made on a further four. Each was a collage of news and views concerning different aspects of life in Ras-Al-Khan. The first programme dealt with the fishing industry, following *hammour, safi* and *sigalee,* a weirdo of the shellfish world, from ocean floor to dinner table. The second delved into the appeal of Arabian perfumes.

The telephone rang as she was checking

background information. 'Alyssa Brett,' she
answered, buried in a reference book.

'Good morning, how are you? Nose to the
grindstone, I trust?'

The unfamiliar drawl made her frown, but
then her brow cleared. This had to be Lennie,
using one of his repertoire of voices. Brilliant at
impersonations which he often incorporated in
his show, he used her as a sounding board. Every
time they spoke over the 'phone he took on a
different character. She had been chatted up by
James Dean, Chinese laundrymen, an irate Welsh
miner searching for a valley, a pseudo Norman
Harding. She was not about to be bamboozled
this time. Lennie, but which character?

'I'm top of the morning,' Alyssa grinned.
'Missing you madly, of course, but at least I have
my work to keep me warm.'

'Missing me?' She heard amusement in his
voice and decided there was a Yorkshire accent in
there somewhere. Who did she know who came
from Yorkshire? Lower lip caught between her
teeth, she tried to work out his adopted persona.
Was this a celebrity, or someone they both knew
in Ras-Al-Khan? 'And what kind of work is
keeping you warm?' he continued.

'Planning a range of programmes for that damn
sheikh.' All thoughts of who Lennie was
supposed to be flew out of the window. 'After
three hours' hard grind last night I'm beginning
to realise what's involved. A hundred and one
sources will need to be contacted, and it looks like
I'll take root in the British Council's research
section. Ferreting out the right people to speak

with might be difficult. And even if I'm fortunate enough to find a decent interpreter, interviews will be complicated by the language barrier. Suppose I come up against red tape? I haven't sussed out the form here yet. And how on earth he expects me to find time to fix appointments between my duties at the news-desk, well ...' She left that problem to be sorted out later. 'Moving around in these temperatures isn't easy. You get fricasseed just waiting for a taxi. Life would be a darn sight simpler if I had my own transport.' Alyssa grinned at the idea. 'Maybe I should demand an interest free loan to buy a Mercedes. What do you think?'

'I think that damn sheikh would say no.'

'Even if I coaxed him?' she asked archly.

'How would you do that?'

'Use your imagination.'

'I don't have any. You tell me,' he ordered.

Alyssa wearied of the game. 'Okay, Lennie, I give up. Who are you?' When there was silence at the other end of the 'phone she quickly became impatient. 'I know it's you, so come clean. Don't waste time, I have work to do. Who are you supposed to be?'

'This is Tariq.'

She gave a disbelieving hoot. 'Not His Excellency Sheikh Tariq bin Hamed Al Zahini? You're losing your touch.'

'I repeat, this is Tariq speaking.'

At first there was a trickle of panic, then a stream, and finally it washed over her in waves. She went hot and cold. Lennie would still be in bed. Her caller *was* the sheikh! The disc jockey could never have reproduced that smoky drawl.

'I'd like to discuss your ideas for new programmes,' the voice continued. 'Would you come along and see me now?'

'I'm sorry. I thought I was speaking to——' she gabbled, ramming apologies down the telephone in frantic dismay.

'*Now*,' he repeated and broke the connection.

Heart quaking, Alyssa collected her papers and somehow managed to reach the boardroom. The knuckles she used to rap on the door were as weak as her knees.

'Come,' a voice ordered, and a dip of his head acknowledged her arrival.

'Good morning, sir.' She was as demure as a schoolgirl. Adding the 'sir' seemed appropriate, because if she was to extricate herself from this *faux pas* she should pay him all the respect he was due.

'Good morning, Mrs Brett.'

What was his mood? Was he angry, about to flail her for impertinence, or would he treat the mistaken identity as a joke? The momentary attention he gave her tremulous smile revealed nothing. Folders crowding the table showed he was deep into the morning's work, so Alyssa sank down, watching as he wrote a margin note in an unhurried hand. He wrote in Arabic, the flowing outlines firm and black on the white page.

He wouldn't dismiss her outright, would he? He was a proud man, all Arabs were, but didn't he have a quirky sense of humour? He would see the funny side—wouldn't he? Alyssa's stomach was packed with heavy chains. What had she said over the 'phone? Desperately she tried to remember, but she felt numb, like a wild animal trapped in car headlights, unable to summon the wit to escape. The sheikh pushed one sheet of paper aside and reached for the next. Did he have her personal file to hand? Had he summoned her in order to make the extravagant and damning gesture of ripping her contract to shreds before her very eyes?

He raised his head, subjecting her to a long hard look which was quite impossible to fathom.

'You never answered my question.'

Alyssa's mind was a blank. 'Your question?'

'You never explained how you intend to coax me into lending you the money to buy a Mercedes.'

Something in his tone unsettled her. Her gaze skittered away. Was he joking? If so, why did the question sound like the herald to sarcastic torture? How was she expected to respond— laugh gaily or offer abject apologies? She risked a look and discovered he was stroking his jaw, waiting for her answer. The slow movement was mesmerising. All she could see was the dark gold of his hands—competent masculine hands with short black hair above the knuckles. Hands eminently suited to wielding a hatchet, or controlling a stallion or fast car with equal ease. Or a woman, she thought, and gave herself a mental shake.

'I didn't mean it,' Alyssa replied breathlessly.

'Didn't mean it? You can't expect me to believe that owning a superb new car wouldn't appeal? I can tell from the way you dress that you're a woman with an unerring eye for the best things in life.'

Her eyes narrowed in alarm. Was he praising or condemning? The gap between their cultures seemed to yawn like the Grand Canyon. Her flair for knowing what people were thinking, and how to handle them, had deserted her. She hadn't a clue what made this man tick, the way his mind worked.

'I wasn't serious. The idea of a loan was a joke. I don't want a car.'

'Don't you?' he drawled, and she recognised from the chill-tempered reply that he was angry, very angry. 'Have the courage of your convictions. Don't be shy, Mrs Brett. Or have you had second thoughts about making love to me?' He had unsheathed an invisible dagger. 'I presume your way of coaxing would be to entice me into your bed and wrap that long blonde hair and those long legs around me? Not a very original ploy, but I'm willing to give it a whirl if you insist. Unfortunately, I can't guarantee a loan for a new car afterwards, that'll depend on your performance.'

Alyssa stared at him in horror. 'You've misunderstood. I don't want a Mercedes, and I don't want——'

'You don't want me?' he finished for her. 'That isn't true. You wanted me the first time you saw me, and I confess the attraction was mutual. I possess what you seem to want—money, and you possess what I desire——'

'You're wrong!' Alyssa stormed from her chair,

the blood coursing through her veins like hot wine. 'You've made a serious error of judgment. Wealth is no aphrodisiac as far as I'm concerned. Just because I happen to be blonde, that doesn't mean I'm a stereotype gold-digger, *Your Excellency*!'

He tossed the fall of his *kaffia* back from a broad shoulder. 'And I, too, am no stereotype,' he rasped. 'I don't go haywire at the twitch of a female rump, nor do I feel it necessary to reward my women with diamond bracelets or Mercedes cars,' he added menacingly. 'I have no intention of being exploited, neither will I allow Ras-Al-Khan's resources to be exploited. You people——'

'I am not you people,' Alyssa insisted, blue eyes blazing. 'I've only been in the Gulf for a short——'

'You people have had things your own way for far too long, but that's to be changed.' He gestured towards her chair. 'Do come and sit down. Shall we make a start? You have my permission to call me Tariq and I'll call you Alyssa, if I may?'

She stared at him, wondering how he could switch from foul insinuations to no-nonsense business meeting in a single breath. Well, his anger may have been appeased, but she still burned with resentment.

'I apologise if I've offended you,' he said, producing a winning smile which confused her further. 'But I find it pays to know exactly where you stand. Isn't it better to clear the air right from day one?' He indicated the papers she had placed on the table. 'Are those your preliminary ideas? May I see them?' Stalking back, she almost flung the notes at him. 'Thank you, Alyssa,' he grinned.

'I hope you can understand them, *Tariq*,' she said icily, damned if she would be wooed. Rich and titled he might be, but he was only a man. A man who had said he was attracted to her. But was he, or had that comment merely been part of his cruel act of discovering exactly where he stood? She was not going to think about that now. All Alyssa knew was that she had coped with Douglas and—so far—with Nigel Dutton, and she would cope with this sheikh, too.

'I'm sure I'll understand,' he said. 'And do calm down.' His grin deepened beneath the black moustache. 'I see you're not a woman for saying, "Yes, sir. No, sir. Three bags full, sir."'

'Do you want me to be?' she demanded.

Tariq laughed. 'Good God, no. I much prefer someone who——' He broke off. 'Are you a passionate lover, Alyssa?'

She gaped, simply gaped. Had he now decided to tease her? Whatever he was doing, he was also making strange things happen to her pulse rate.

She gulped in a breath. 'I don't know.'

'You can't have reached the great age of twenty-seven without discovering whether or not you're passionate,' he chided, his eyes sparkling.

Alyssa knew she must play it cool—as cool as possible, under the circumstances. 'Yes, I suppose I am, and how did you know I'm twenty-seven?'

Tariq was silken. 'I've read your file, as I've read all the personnel files. I'm aware you began your career in hospital radio, that you were widowed less than a year ago, and——' The grin was extinguished, the sensual prankster disappeared. 'And I also know you're capable of far more than the newscasting and other bits and pieces which you're presently contributing to Radio Ras-Al-Khan.'

The door had been slammed on personal conversation. Now he perused her notes, asked scalpel-sharp questions, listened intently to replies before asking further questions. Some of her ideas he accepted, others were rejected as being too radical for a Muslim country. Time passed, and Alyssa began to relax for somewhere along the way Tariq had learned the knack of putting people at their ease when it suited him. The world of radio absorbed them both, made them equals, and the sticky start to the meeting was forgotten.

'Do you smoke?' he asked, allowing the pace to slacken as midday approached. Alyssa shook her head. 'Mind if I do?'

'Please, carry on.'

'I kicked the habit three years ago—so I thought—but since arriving in the Gulf I've started again. Nerves, I guess.' Nerves! she thought, as he selected a black Sobranie from his cigarette case. He doesn't have a single nerve in his entire body. 'Sorry if I'm driving hard,' Tariq continued, narrowing his eyes against the drifting smoke, 'but six weeks is all I've been given to knock things into shape.'

'And then you return to the oil scene?'

'Not exactly return, because I haven't given up

the reins. I'm intending to juggle oil and radio together for six weeks—though not a minute longer.' His smile was self-mocking. 'You see before you one of those work-orientated guys, an over-achiever.'

Alyssa was intrigued. 'Did you offer your services to Radio Ras-Al-Khan or were you . . . pushed?'

'Pushed, by my grandfather. He's very much aware of the influence the media can have on a society, and is eager for progress. And when he's eager, he's eager. Ideally qualified nationals should be running the local radio and television, but,' Tariq gave a teasing glance, 'as that can't happen overnight you expatriates are a necessary evil.'

'Thank you,' she said pertly, and laughed.

'We do have people being trained in mass media, both here and abroad, but it'll take a few years for them to graduate.'

'And until then you're lumbered with folk like me?' Alyssa suggested, prompting him to spread his hands in a gesture of wry defeat. 'Where did you study the media?'

'I have no formal training,' he confessed, 'but luckily my mind's like a sponge. I seem able to soak up information and squeeze it out later.' This was no boast, merely a flat statement which she saw no reason to contradict. His knowledge of radio had been sturdy and complete. 'I was close to a top television producer in New York for a couple of years,' he explained. 'And I paid attention. If you come from a developing country like Ras-Al-Khan, then it's wise to be on the alert

for what can be learned from established
procedures.'

'And your friend, he took you though the radio
stations, too?'

Tariq looked past her, then returned his eyes to
her face. 'Yes, but my friend was a she. I drove
her wild, asking so many questions. She reckoned
work, be it oil, the media, or whatever, gave me
my highs.' He threw back his head and laughed.
'But maybe not all of them. There's enough of
the harem master in me to appreciate the
pleasures of the flesh.'

The dark brown eyes caught hers and Alyssa's
heart began to thump. Since Douglas's death all
thoughts of lovemaking had been stashed away in
a sealed box in her mind—until she had met
Tariq. He had said she had wanted him when she
had first set eyes on him, and he had been right.
That giddy feeling, the heated rush of blood
below the surface of her skin, had been a purely
sexual reaction. She frowned, distressed he
should possess the power to excite her in this
way.

'How do you come to have a Yorkshire accent?'
she enquired, meeting his look with purposeful
neutrality. 'It's slight, but I noticed it over the
'phone.'

'My mother comes from Yorkshire.' He
noticed her surprise. 'Didn't you realise I'm a
mongrel? I was under the impression at least
fifty per cent of the expatriate community's
gossip centred on the affairs of the Al Zahini
family.'

He had distanced himself from her. Alyssa was

back to being classified as one of 'you people' and she didn't like it.

'I don't listen to gossip,' she told him tartly.

'No yackety-yack beside the pool?'

'None. And I don't spend all my free time sunbathing,' she insisted, defending herself against the slight jeer, the faint reproof.

'Maybe not.' Tariq's gaze travelled across her honeyed arms with their shimmer of down. 'How do you fill your free time, Alyssa?'

Inconsequential though it was, she found herself noticing how he pronounced her name. It rolled from between his lips like a love chant.

'Just lately I've been recording special sound effects. There weren't any on tape, and I thought the studio could use a selection.'

'Makes sense.'

'And I'm also involved with typing out a play of Brough's.'

'He writes plays? Is it good?'

Alyssa laughed. 'How do I know? I'm not a drama critic.'

'You're not stupid, either. Would the play be suitable for transmission in Ras-Al-Khan, on radio or television?'

'Possibly, but——'

'Ask Brough to let me see a copy on completion, if he's agreeable.'

'He'll be agreeable,' she said, the speed at which Tariq reached decisions making her smile. 'Allow his play to be produced and he'll be your friend for life.'

'Good. It'd be a bonus if someone didn't cast me in the role of exterminator. I'm not here to destroy, I'm here to create, but time's short so I must move quickly. If toes get trampled on in the process, then hard luck. I would hope people here are mature enough to realise what I'm trying to do.'

'I think they are—mostly,' Alyssa amended, recalling Lennie's determination to go his own way regardless.

'So they'll all be my friends——' a brow lifted, '—including you?'

Some inflexion in his question made her nerve ends tingle, and it became imperative she place their relationship on a strictly business footing.

'Why not? We both want Radio Ras-Al-Khan to produce entertainment and information which will stimulate the public. Our aim is to help people to widen their horizons and fulfil their talents?'

Alyssa caught the flicker of a grin. 'That sounds very earnest, but I suppose you're right.'

'I am.'

'Which means we can work together as friends?'

'Yes.'

'Good friends?'

Why was he so persistent? She didn't understand the point he was trying to make.

'*Yes.*'

'Platonic friends?' Tariq drawled.

'Naturally!'

'Then how do you dispose of the sexual excitement which exists between us?'

Once again she gaped. Why must he be so

blunt? How could he mention sex so easily, so calmly? Was this another test like before?

'Nothing exists between us,' she blurted. 'Besides, I understand you're about to be married to a cousin, one of Sheikh Suroor's daughters.'

'And I understood you were too busy to listen to gossip?' came the stinging backhander. Alyssa had hit a raw patch. 'I suggest you get your facts straight. Religious differences have yet to be reconciled before Shamsa and I are engaged.' Tariq took his time to straighten a stack of folders. 'Don't misunderstand me. I wasn't suggesting any kind of liaison. I was merely being honest about——' He struck away what came next with an abrupt jerk of his hand. 'The last thing I need is you in my bed.'

'And it's the last thing you'll get,' she returned, furious at the assumption she might willingly go there.

'Would it be so dreadful?' he asked, then frowned, to become the efficient business tycoon again. 'Thank you for your time. Our meeting has been both instructive and constructive.'

And *de*structive, Alyssa thought, hastily gathering up her papers.

'You have permission to go ahead with the first two programmes, as outlined. Expenses may be claimed, reasonable expenses for taxis and such.' As he raised his head from stuffing documents into his briefcase, there was humour in his eyes. 'But don't waste your time submitting a bill for a Mercedes because that damn sheikh——'

'I won't,' she promised, and could not stop a smile in return.

How could Tariq have her so alarmed one moment and the next reduce her to benign acquiescence? She had prided herself on her ability to remain cool and composed whatever the situation, so why did she now feel as if she was riding a roller-coaster, no handed?

'Are you satisfied with the deal you're getting from Radio Ras-Al-Khan?' Tariq asked, as they left the boardroom and headed down the stairs.

'Very much so. The salary's fantastic,' Alyssa could not help adding.

'There are more important things in life than money,' he commented.

The blunt certainty of his tone suddenly made her want to ball her fists and scream. What did he know? How could Tariq ever guess at the agony of having every penny you earned today—and for the next three years—already committed?

'Have you ever scrimped and saved?' she asked archly.

She was given a long cool look. 'No.'

'Or lain awake night after night, wondering where the next pound was coming from?'

'No.'

'Then I'd be grateful if you wouldn't be so damned patronising,' Alyssa said bitterly. 'Believe me, money is important, ultra important. Have money and you automatically have protection, freedom, self-respect. Without it you—you——'

She stopped short. Hinting at her problems was insane. Thankfully she realised they had reached the studio door and she turned, desperate to escape. In a few minutes' time she would be reading the lunchtime news. But as she turned, cool fingers caught at her wrist.

'Whatever's made you so uptight about money?' Tariq questioned.

'It wasn't whatever, it was whoever.' She snatched her hand away. 'And the answer to that is my husband and a man called Nigel Dutton!'

CHAPTER FOUR

NAMING names had not been so much insane as suicidal. Terrified he might start asking questions, Alyssa had shot off and spent the rest of the day worrying herself sick. How could she explain away her outburst? Not easily. Tariq was astute, too astute. Her only hope was that the disclosures would fall from his consciousness as rapidly as she had pushed them in. When he had rung down a couple of mornings later to discuss a programming point, she had felt groggy. But he had kept strictly to business and she had realised, with a dizzying sense of relief, that he had not considered her exposé significant. She was safe.

As one week became two, Tariq began to drum up what had seemed impossible beneath Mr Harding's control—enthusiasm within the broadcasting personnel. The initial grumbles and threats of mutiny had faded, and compliments began to circulate. Admittedly they were grudging, but Alyssa knew they would become sincere once it was realised that taking a pride in your work meant going home at night with a warm glow of satisfaction. Of course, there had to be someone who swam against the tide, and that someone had to be Lennie. He skidded from brash rebellion to uneasy compliance, yet had rare moments of what appeared to be admiration.

For herself, Alyssa found the sheikh's

dynamism infectious. Since he had given the go-ahead, her own pace had shot off into a gallop. There was no more frustration, no more hanging around drinking endless cups of coffee. Now she was busy from morning to night, for in addition to her regular newscasting she was occupied making 'phone calls, checking facts, gobbling up the history of the Gulf, searching for elusive snippets of interest. One idea led to another, and she became so engrossed in structuring her programmes that little time was left over in which to worry about Nigel Dutton.

'What's next in your programme about the fishing industry?' Tariq enquired. They were in the boardroom, deep into one of their regular discussions.

'I need to speak to some fishermen, but for that an interpreter's required. Do you think there's a chance I'd find a local woman who could help?'

His brow creased. 'Why a woman?'

'Because I haven't spoken to a single female citizen of Ras-Al-Khan since I arrived here, and I'd sorely like to redress the balance.'

'Sorry, but your luck's out. Very few local women work, something in the region of two per cent.'

'They prefer to stay at home?'

Tariq nodded. 'But don't imagine they're meek little creatures. My sister-in-law's a sparky——' He broke off, as though abruptly aware of betraying confidences to an employee. Of late he had been breaking off statements with increasing regularity, and Alyssa understood. She was confused about their relationship herself. On one level they were contemporaries, thinking along the same lines, using the same language, yet on another they were worlds apart. At times she forgot he was a man separated from her by race, rank and power, and used a straightforward approach. Who was Tariq—a young European male or an Arab sheikh? It was difficult to tell. 'As regards an interpreter,' he continued, 'I have a second cousin who's eager to practise his English. Let me know when and where you need help, and I'll rustle up Abdullah.' He paused. 'The boy's eighteen and has a weakness for blue-eyed blondes, so go easy.'

Because he had spoken without humour, Alyssa's hackles began to rise. 'Are you frightened I might seduce him?' she challenged.

'There's more danger of Abdullah seducing you,' he said flatly. 'But I don't want him to do anything foolish, like falling in love with a foreigner.'

'Why ever not?' she enquired icily, tempted to point out he was half a despised foreigner himself. But, of course, the Tariq who spoke to her now was every inch an Arab!

'Because he's due to be married next year.'

'An arranged marriage?'

'That is the custom.'

'Are *all* marriages in Ras-Al-Khan arranged?' Alyssa enquired in clipped tones.

He read her mind. 'Do you consider I'm the kind of man who'd allow someone else to choose his bride for him?'

She could not answer that. Did he mean his marriage to Shamsa had not been arranged, that he had conveniently plumped for his cousin himself?

'Tell me something.' Tariq subjected her to a piercing look. 'Why did you choose to come and work in Ras-Al-Khan?'

'I—er—for experience,' she stammered, full of apprehension. Alyssa found her fingers moving to fuss with the ribboned neckline of her vanilla-coloured dress.

'But choosing to work for what's almost an embryo radio station doesn't make sense from the point of view of your career,' he said, lifting his gold cigarette lighter and weighing it first in one hand and then in the other.

'I wanted to broaden my horizons,' she countered.

'You don't broaden your horizons by steering into a backwater. When you add Radio Ras-Al-Khan to your *curriculum vitae* nobody's going to shout hosannas.'

Clearly he had a point, but Alyssa was not about to admit to anything which might incriminate her.

'Working here is a challenge,' she declared. 'It's totally different to anything I've done before and I'm enjoying the experience of living abroad. Ever since I was a child I've loved to travel, to see new places, meet new people, and——'

'Would you kindly stop having a conversation with yourself and answer my question. Cut out the . . .' a dark gold hand sliced the air, 'flannel!'

'I wanted to earn money, good money,' she rattled off, seeing no alternative but to tell him the truth.

'That's what Jerry Thompson said.'

'You've spoken to Jerry?' Her blue eyes widened in alarm.

'Yes, his name was in your file as a reference, so I called him yesterday. I've been trying to figure out why you came here because you're streets ahead of the rest.' Tariq ditched the lighter. 'Let's take it from the top. As a radio boss Norman Harding has as much pizzaz as the average dormouse.'

'I don't understand why he's been allowed to function on half-throttle all these years,' she interrupted, seeing a chance to steer the conversation on to safer ground.

'That's because until recently no one among Ras-Al-Khan's hierarchy has had the broadcasting know-how to realise just how mediocre he is. And, let's face it, there've been more pressing matters than radio to be dealt with. The boom-town growth has meant there are not enough nationals with the proper skills. Expatriates have been brought in to fill the gaps, but some haven't done their jobs as they should. Matters are being sorted out, but it takes time.'

'There's a rumour going the rounds about Mr Harding taking early retirement,' she said, determined to keep the pot boiling.

'He needs more time to sail his boat.' A scornful brow lifted. 'He's being replaced by a national, Mohammed Nasser. Mohammed's worked with the BBC for the past six years in various parts of the world, so he's experienced. He starts a two-month takeover period this week.' Tariq continued his countdown. 'Brough Maury's a regular guy who works well under guidance, but who'll never aspire to the heights. Lennie . . .' He paused. 'Now he's a special case. He has the ability to be top-class if his temperament doesn't get in the way, but— Every time Mr Leith smiles I freeze, waiting for him to kick me in the groin. Incidentally, I've arranged for his programmes to be monitored. He does have a tendency to allow that acid tongue of his to go too far, and should he step out of line . . .'

The threat was left hanging, but Alyssa could guess what would happen. If the disc jockey stepped too far out of line, the next steps he took would be through the airport—outward bound.

'Lennie'd be okay if—if he could be made to see sense,' she protested, adopting the protective role she had adopted so often in the past on her husband's behalf.

'And how does that happen?' She had to confess she did not know. 'So we're back to you,' Tariq said. 'Jerry Thompson assured me you're creative, reliable and proficient, which I already know. He reckoned that if you'd worked for his London team as he wanted, you could have reached the top of the radio tree. You've got what it takes. In many ways you remind me of Lauren.'

'Lauren?' she echoed.

'The televison producer I told you about.'

'Oh.'

'Don't say "Oh" like that,' he retorted.

'Like what?'

'As though you don't approve. Lauren was a very smart lady. Everyone admired her dedication and down-to-earth approach. Yes,' he mused, embarking on a nostalgia kick, 'it was that which attracted me in the first place. She made it plain she didn't give a damn about my status or my wealth. *And* she was refreshing because she never once tried to use me.'

'Other people do?' she questioned.

'*Did*. I'm too long in the tooth to be fooled now, but when I was younger——' His lip curled dismissively. 'You've no idea of the types who regard a man like me as heaven sent.' The scour of his eyes made Alyssa wonder if he was warning her off. 'There was a time when I thought that when I married my bride would come from the West, but now I realise I must take a bride from Ras-Al-Khan.' Tariq flicked his dark gold fingers. 'East and West are poles apart. Totally incompatible.'

The remark stung. She felt it was patently untrue. And how could he reconcile his statement with the mix of Western and Eastern blood which flowed through his veins? What was he trying to prove?

'But we function well together in harness,' she protested, then thought it prudent to add, 'in radio terms.'

'To a point,' he said, with a shrug.

'Aren't you contradicting yourself?' Alyssa demanded. 'You say East and West are incompatible, yet you were . . . close to Lauren.'

'That was in the past.'

'But now your eyes have been opened?' she asked tartly.

Tariq resumed his weighing of the cigarette

lighter. 'Jerry reckoned you were committing career suicide by burying yourself out here.'

'Nonsense. In Ras-Al-Khan I'll be able to broaden my horizons,' she repeated, disconcerted by this abrupt switch in the conversation. What else had Jerry said? To have been discussed made her uneasy, yet Jerry had no inkling of the true reason why she had had to turn down his offer of employment. 'And I'll meet people from different countries, learn about different lifestyles.'

'The salary's the real draw?' Tariq insisted, his frown indicating she was waffling. 'Yet you wouldn't have been a pauper in London. Your rate of pay would've been high for a woman in her twenties.'

'I needed more,' she mumbled, finding a sudden fascination in a felt tip pen. 'You wouldn't understand.'

'Wouldn't I?'

For a hare-brained split second she wondered if he would, then gave a brittle laugh. 'I doubt it.'

'Try me.'

Alyssa refused to respond to his appeal. 'No, thank you.' She used her steadiest, coolest voice. 'As you've pointed out, East and West are poles apart. On certain subjects you and I—well!' She rolled her eyes with theatrical effect.

The muscle which clenched in his jaw showed Tariq resented being brushed off. He was ready to protest, when a knock on the door deflected his attention.

'*Ta'ala*,' he commanded, and grinned when a robed, blackbearded man strode in. Alyssa recognised the newcomer as his brother, Sheikh Karim.

'I've tracked you down at last,' Karim teased, and the two men hugged each other in a spontaneous display of affection.

Such uncomplicated good humour was touching. If only her relationships were so warm, Alyssa thought, watching on enviously. But a wall of pretence separated her from Meg, the sister she loved so dearly, and all rapport with her mother had disappeared long ago. When her mother had remarried after years of widowhood, the teenaged Alyssa had been happy to welcome her stepfather into the family, but how different her mother's response had been to Douglas. *He* had not been welcomed. Her mother had been strongly critical, forecasting trouble and thus alienating the young couple. And even now, almost a year since his death, she had still not been able to find a good word for him.

'I trust my brother hasn't been lashing the whip too severely?' Karim asked her, when introductions had been made. His dark eyes twinkled. 'I fear Tariq can be a hard taskmaster.'

'I'm surviving—no weals, so far,' Alyssa grinned, deciding she could grow to like Sheikh Karim. He was a stately figure, but affected no airs or graces.

'I believe you're organising a series of programmes centred on Ras-Al-Khan?' he smiled. 'Do tell me about them.'

She was busy explaining the format when a boy arrived bearing a coffee pot brimming with the cardamom-flavoured brew, and a supply of tiny handleless cups.

'Thank goodness someone can spare the time to put me in the picture,' Karim joked. 'When Tariq became a member of my household I innocently imagined long leisurely conversations in the evenings, but he prefers to devote his time to intercourse with the telex machine.' He regarded his brother with grave eyes. 'Man was not meant to work twenty-four hours a day. When you take a wife, you must change your ways. No woman will——'

'Is there anything further you'd like to ask Mrs Brett?' came the interruption. 'She's a busy person, and we've taken up enough of her time as it is.'

The dismissal was blatant. Sheikh Karim suggested she might care for a cup of coffee, but Alyssa demurred and beat a hasty retreat.

What she would give to be able to switch off the alarm, roll over and go back to sleep. But rising at the crack of dawn seemed to be her destiny. Even this morning, the one day in the week when her radio duties didn't start until noon, Alyssa found herself tiptoeing past the porter who slumbered at the Colonnade's reception desk.

'We'll collect you at five-thirty, sharp,' Byron had said.

A scarf covering jumbo rollers, she stood on the topmost marble step and scanned to left and right. A first glance through the dawn haze convinced her she was the only person in the sheikhdom who was up and alert—well, nearly alert. She yawned, waited, and inspected her watch. Almost a quarter to six. Looking on the bright side, at least no one she knew was around; though a few trucks, loaded with labourers, were starting to roll by. This Alyssa Brett, hair sausage-wrapped, face shining, was a far cry from the well-groomed young woman who read the news. The purple caftan and thongs which completed the picture would never get her into the list of the World's Ten Best-Dressed Women!

Ten-to-six, and a drop of perspiration slid down her neck. Dawn it might be, but summer temperatures in the Gulf rarely fell below the high eighties, night or day. Pin in her mouth as she tightened a roller, Alyssa recalled the photographer's stipulation that her hair was to be a 'gloriously exotic lion's mane'. If Byron didn't hurry all he would find would be cats' tails!

Her spirits lifted when a small bus trundled from the horizon and coughed to a halt before her. Inside languished two other models, Ophelia-type brunettes, pale of face and large of eye. Byron, a reed-thin figure in tangerine, shouted hello, as did the boutique's co-ordinator and a plump American matron who named herself as 'surrogate Mom, head cook and bottle washer'. Alyssa struggled inside and off the bus puffed, to eventually deposit them at the harbour.

Shrouded in early, morning mist, the workaday wharves had been transformed into a mystical land of half hidden silhouettes and pale blurred shapes. A gap in the haze, and distant onion-shaped domes of a mosque drifted into view. A solitary seabird wheeled low, searching for a fish breakfast. Alyssa paused, listening to the phut-phut of an invisible *abra*, one of the small ferry boats which shipped workers across the water.

'Hurry, hurry,' Byron yelled, leaping around checking dials and peering down viewfinders. 'This light won't last.'

Up the gang plank on to the wooden-hulled *dhow* which had been requisitioned as changing quarters and backdrop, everyone went.

'The places we're expected to operate from!' grumbled Chrissy, one of the Ophelia girls, when below decks proved to be dark, smelly and hot. 'What *have* the sailors been doing down here?'

Alyssa changed into the African-printed bermudas and matching top provided, and waited her turn for the crate which served as make-up chair. Her face crayoned, she switched to another up-turned crate where the surrogate Mom undid her rollers and brushed out her hair.

'Look at you, honey, a jungle maiden as Byron ordered,' the woman grinned, and the mirror showed that despite the clammy heat her hair rampaged lion-like around her shoulders.

Whatever Byron wanted, Byron made sure he got, and the first tentative moments when Alyssa felt camera-shy rapidly dissolved. Too busy obeying his commands to be self-conscious, she found herself with limbs draped along the prow, standing smartly to attention beside the wheel-house door, sitting crosslegged on bales of psychedelic mattresses which made up part of the *dhow*'s motley cargo. Within half an hour the first reel of photographs had been taken, and she forgave the photographer for his late arrival.

Byron was a shrewd exponent of his craft, treating
each frame like a work of art. He was sensitive to
a curl of mist, a spontaneous arch of limb or
shoulder, to the weather-worn texture of the deck
timbers. Reels of film later and the mist
evaporated. Pearl-grey sky deepened into blue.
The harbour rubbed its eyes and came awake.

At first a gaggle of sailors on an adjacent boat
took an interest, then other men sloped up, dark-
skinned and exotically tribal in robes and a
variety of headdresses. A group of small boys
joined in, squatting on their haunches to view the
proceedings. Cars stopped, heads craned from
windows, office workers made a detour.

'Change of mood now,' crooned Byron, when
the final change into multi-coloured maillots
was made. 'Seduction time. Sprawl your lovely
limbs on those mattresses and think sexy
thoughts.' He bent to fluff Alyssa's hair around
her shoulders. 'Fantasise about some macho guy
who's ridden in from the desert and who's
thirsting for——'

His voice faded as she lay back on her elbows
and surrendered to a hot wash of excitement.
Imagine Tariq, riding on a black stallion. She
could see him in her mind's eye. A fierce wind
would plaster his robes against his chest, outline
the solid energy of his thighs. He would leap
from the horse and gather her up. Carrying her to
a tent, womb-like and secure, he would hold her
close and slowly undress her, making long
delicious love.

'Get a move on.' Byron prodded with his foot.
'It's drink and dancing next,' he explained, as

Alyssa leapt up, red-faced and bemused. Thinking thoughts like those was dangerous. 'Pretend it's champagne, the real thing,' he encouraged, as tall glasses were filled with soda water and handed around.

The surrogate Mom produced a portable radio and spun the dial to full volume. The harbour reverberated to the latest electronic rock. As Alyssa and her partners began to dance, the crowd cheered. She swung her hips and took a sip of the ice-cold soda water. It felt like nectar to her parched throat. She gulped down one helping and asked for a refill, giggling when the bubbles fizzed up her nose. The second glass was almost drained when Chrissy, beside her, gave a sharp intake of breath.

'I don't like to worry you,' the girl hissed from the corner of her mouth. 'But do you see that big blue car? There aren't any number plates, so chances are it belongs to a member of the ruling family. Seems the aristocracy has caught our little act. There'll be hell to pay. Byron, Byron, stop everything!' she yelped, but the photographer was occupied lining up the next shot and took no notice.

Following Chrissy's nod, Alyssa looked beyond the crowd to the road which divided the wharves from the business district of Ras-Al-Khan and managed to pick out a navy-blue BMW parked against the kerb. Behind tinted windows she saw the indistinct outline of a man in white robes.

'Any idea who it is?' she hissed back.

''Fraid not. Could be His Excellency Sheikh Ahmad for all I know. Byron, Byron,' Chrissy yelped again, waving a frantic hand which this time stopped him in his tracks, 'we're being watched.'

'Not the police?' Having picked up her urgency, Byron was yelping, too.

'No, some local bigwig, and maybe that's worse!'

Chaos reigned. Abandoning his camera, the photographer hustled the three girls down into the cabin where he began buttering thick assurances of 'No problem, no problem,' on to their dismay.

'Probably just some young sheikh who appreciates the female form. You'll have made his day.'

'Huh! I'll remember to tell that to the judge when he's deciding whether my jail term should be three years or six,' jeered Chrissy, flinging on clothes as fast as she could.

Jail term! Alyssa felt faint. Among his threats that of a jail sentence had been one of Nigel Dutton's favourites, but not in Ras-Al-Khan, too? She had always prided herself on being a law-abiding citizen, yet fate seemed determined to put her behind bars one way or another. She visualised how they must have looked—three European girls in revealing swimsuits gyrating before a crowd of ogling Middle-Eastern males. Her doubts about taking on this modelling job had been proved correct. She should have followed her gut instinct and to hell with extra earnings. She had been a fool to say yes, especially knowing Byron to be one of Lennie's madcap friends. Only the other evening Brough had voiced misgivings about her wisdom in becoming involved in 'Lennie's circuit' as he called it, and Tariq had clearly stated his opinion of moonlighting. Why hadn't she listened?

Alyssa jammed her rollers into her totebag. If the Arab behind the tinted windows had been Tariq, what then? How would he react? Would he terminate her contract? Surely he wouldn't have her flung into jail? Yet what better way of proving his allegiance to Arabian ideals than having a white girl punished for breaking the social code!

If only she could remember the make of car he drove. But Tariq would not waste his time by stopping to watch a sideshow, would he? He was a man of action, not a voyeur. He had told her his highs came from business. But not all of them! Her stomach churned. He might be aloof now, but sometimes when he looked at her Tariq was one hundred per cent the hungry male. His head might tell him Western women no longer appealed, but his glands disagreed. A certain chemistry *did* exist. He could deny compatibility until kingdom come, but that abstract zing was ever-present in the air. They seemed to have an uncontrollable penchant for making each other sexually alert.

Simmer down and be logical, Alyssa told herself. For a start the ruling family encompasses a vast number of people—distant relatives, minor sheikhs who are cousins of cousins of cousins. And they are not the only ones who drive unmarked vehicles, high-ranking government officials also have that privilege. The BMW could belong to any one of two or three hundred people. How ridiculous to jump to the immediate conclusion that Tariq had to be the one sitting inside. As Byron had said, the spectator could easily be some boy who would treat the whole thing as a lark.

Emerging on deck, Alyssa searched the roadside but the car had gone. The crowd also began to disappear now that the dancing girls were a thing of the past. Vehicles sped away, sailors returned to their chores, small boys ran off giggling. By the time they climbed back into the bus the harbour was operating as normal.

CHAPTER FIVE

TAKING her place at the microphone to read the noon news bulletin, Alyssa felt as if she had already completed a day's work. The bulletin over, she taped a number of time checks and dealt with an early afternoon short story, but the race of adrenalin through her bloodstream was beginning to slow. An extended news round-up at six and a short bulletin at closedown lay ahead. So far as immediates were concerned, she was not under pressure, yet progress must be made on her fish programme. In the presenters' lounge she had lifted the telephone, intending to ring around some hotels to see if a chef or two could be sweet-talked into contributing his favourite seafood recipe, when Brough walked in.

'What do you think about a radio poetry spot?' he asked, perching on the corner of the desk. 'I wanted to mention the idea to Tariq, but he's tied up with some oil crisis today and hasn't been in. So what's your opinion? You see, I've been discussing readings with a guy I know from the amateur dramatic society and——'

For a full quarter of an hour, he spoke nonstop. Alyssa's eyes glazed, grew heavy. She tried to stop a yawn and couldn't, not that Brough noticed. He droned on and on and on. Fortunately he did not require much feedback, and her nod at the end of his recital was treated as adequate confirmation that he was on the right track. He grinned farewell and disappeared. As her eyelids persisted in drooping, she rested her head on her arms and promised herself a short rest—just a catnap.

The telephone shrilled in her ear, as loud and scary as a police siren. Startled, Alyssa was snatched from being fast asleep to being wide awake. She lunged an arm across the desk, searching for the receiver and knocking papers askew in her haste.

'Hello?' she gasped, gazing at her watch and forcing her eyes to focus. Why didn't the fingers make sense? Good grief, it was five-thirty. She had been asleep for almost two hours, and there seemed a distinct possibility that, left undisturbed, she would have slept on through the six o'clock news round-up!

'This is His Excellency Sheikh Tariq's secretary speaking,' an accented voice informed her. 'His Excellency wishes to see you at the coast palace this evening, so a car will collect you from the radio complex at six thirty-five. May I advise my master that you will be able to keep this appointment?'

'Er—yes.'

'His Excellency looks forward to your visit.'

When the line went dead, Alyssa replaced the receiver and frowned. Her fears about Tariq having been in the navy limousine flooded back. Had he watched? Yes. No. Maybe. Tormented with indecision, it needed all the control of a professional to get her through reading the news, and then it was six thirty-five.

A white-robed man in a lacy skull cap waited for her beside a gleaming bronze Mercedes. He bowed low as she approached, opening wide the rear door. As they set off, Alyssa's precariously assembled poise began to melt. Soon she was soggy with problems. Why hadn't Tariq spoken to her himself over the telephone? Why must she report to the palace in person? What was so important that it couldn't wait until tomorrow? An old fear was resurrected. Had he decided she was dispensable? Praised her work he had, but also he had spoken of part-time staffing, stressing the economies which could be made there. And only last week a woman with wide experience of American radio had written in, requesting a few hours' work each day. Once Tariq reached a decision, he lost no time setting it in motion. If he had decided to trim the payroll by substituting part-time staff, what could she do?

'Be happy,' coaxed the driver, smiling through the mirror.

Alyssa forced a grin, and tried to think what to say. 'It's been a very hot day,' she said, somewhat foolishly.

'Better here in winter.'

It was obvious he wanted to talk, so she asked a question about the camel racing which took place in Ras-Al-Khan during the cooler weather. Despite his poor English and her virtually nonexistent Arabic, somehow a fair amount of information was exchanged, and their conversation only ended when they arrived at the splendid black-and-gold gates of the coast palace.

Turbanned guards sprang to the alert, and as

the Mercedes moved forward Alyssa saw they
had entered another world. The concrete and
dusty industry of the city had been left behind.
Sculptured green lawns rolled to left and right,
and among frangipani trees rose fountains,
cooling the air. When the car rounded a bend, her
eyes opened wide. Ahead lay a shining white
palace—a slice of pure Eastern romance, with
graceful shaded arcades and decorated pillars.
Black wrought iron balconies punctuated pristine
walls on the upper floor.

Braking beneath a portico where jasmine
clambered in profusion, the driver handed her
into the care of a manservant who had noiselessly
appeared. With a bow of his head he indicated
she should follow, and led the way between heavy
teak doors. Alyssa absorbed no more than a cool
entrance hall, its white marble floor gilded by the
rays of the setting sun, before they were out again
into the balmy air. They crossed a courtyard,
heavy with the perfume of orange blossom, then
went beneath a flowered pergola where the chant
of cicadas filled her ears. Next she was led
through another cool hall. The palace was a
sprawling labyrinth of low buildings interwoven
with courtyards, and soon they skirted what
appeared to be the family domain. A pedal car
and bicycle lay in a corner and, making mute
reference, the servant held down a hand to
indicate a small child, smiling at her over his
shoulder. This palace—home of Sheikh Karim
and his family—was a happy place, Alyssa
thought, hearing a burst of childish laughter in
the distance.

They entered a separate wing, where the servant halted to rap on a polished door.

'*Ta'ala*,' came the command.

Recognising the low rich voice, all her fears about dismissal and the modelling fiasco came back into sharp clarity. Alyssa had an urge to take to her heels and run, but instead she took a deep breath and walked forward.

'Good evening, Mrs Brett,' Tariq said stiffly, rising to greet her from behind a wide desk.

'Good evening.'

Her reply was automatic, for surprise had whisked away reasoned thought. Tariq was wearing Western clothes! Nonplussed to find him in an expensively tailored cream suit, with peat-brown shirt and toning tie, she stood mute as he gave instructions to the servant. The man retreated, quietly closing the door behind him, and still she gaped.

'What do you think you were doing this morning?' he demanded, each word sharp as a razor. In the servant's presence he had been a well-schooled lamb, now he was a panther, stalking its pray.

'You saw me?' she croaked, then clearing her throat. 'It was you in the BMW?'

Tariq's eyes glittered dangerously as he gave a terse nod. 'And you were damned lucky it *was* me.'

'Lucky? Why?'

Alyssa did not feel the least bit lucky, not with him glaring like that. He took a menacing stride forwards and then another, forcing her to step back until she found herself trapped against the wall with no place else to go. They were in an office. Together with a bank of filing cabinets, there was a photocopier, telex machine and a shredder. A desk, bearing piles of folders, sat before a window, now covered with the beige vertical slats of a blind, but which must overlook a courtyard.

'You were lucky only I was on hand to watch you breaking the law!' he stormed, leaning over her. 'If the police, or someone else in authority, had witnessed such a flagrant defiance, you'd have been hauled into court and promptly punished. It would have meant prison or deportation, or both.'

'But plenty of girls wear swimsuits on the beaches or around the pools,' she defended, clutching her shoulder bag at her waist, using it as a barrier. Tariq was much too close for comfort.

'You can't compare sunbathing in relative privacy to displaying yourself in a busy port before an audience of hundreds, all male,' he snapped.

Alyssa summoned up her courage. She refused to sink into oblivion, just to suit *him*. 'I displayed myself, as you call it, for only a few minutes, and I never realised modelling swimwear could be construed as breaking the rules until ...' she sighed, 'it was too late.' She rallied, trying to sound cool and reasonable. 'But prison or deportation seem barbaric punishments for such a small misdemeanour.'

'Don't act dumb! And don't hold this thing as though you're about to use it as a battering ram,' he raged, snatching her bag from her and tossing it on to a nearby chair.

The loss took on the form of a psychological disaster and left Alyssa floundering. She felt as if she had been set adrift on the sea of his anger, and all she had to cling on to was faith in her own judgment—a very wavery faith. She attempted to structure a defence.

'I realise that in the Middle East women are expected to dress and act with decorum, but there's obviously a very thin line between right and wrong. I agree appearing in a swimsuit at the harbour was . . .' she rummaged in her mind for the right word, '. . . unwise, but I still consider you are over-reacting. We were on deck for only——'

'The swimsuit comes second.' Tariq spat out each word from between clenched teeth. 'It was the drinking which was illegal.'

'The drinking?' she queried with a frown.

He raked a hand through his hair, tumbling dark strands across his brow. 'For heaven's sake, Alyssa, you must know that blatant public consumption of alcohol in a Muslim country is strictly against the law. Ras-Al-Khan may be liberal in that foreigners are allowed liquor licences so that they can drink at home. And admittedly there are bars in hotels. But to flaunt alcohol in front of a bunch of uneducated dockers! You were violating all the rules.'

She looked blank. 'What alcohol?'

With a snarl of rage he grabbed her wrists, yanking her arms above her head so that he had savagely shackled her to the wall.

'The champagne,' he rasped. 'Do you imagine it went unnoticed?'

His face was inches from hers, so close she could feel the heat of his breath against her cheek, smell the woody essence of his aftershave. Alyssa struggled to free herself, but he allowed no escape.

'But we didn't drink champagne,' she protested. 'All we had was soda water.'

Tariq's brow creased. 'Soda water?'

'Yes. The other two models and I drank soda water from champagne glasses.' His surprise gave an unexpected advantage and provided Alyssa with the bravado to challenge him. She stared steadfastly back into his eyes. 'Ask Byron, ask other members of the team. Check with the bystanders. If you hadn't been watching through tinted glass you would've been able to spot the difference yourself. Despatch a messenger to the *dhow* and I'm sure he'll be able to bring back the empty bottles as proof positive.' Her cheeks were flushed, her breasts rising and falling with offended pride. 'And now if you would be so kind as to release me?' she demanded, every quivering inch the haughty duchess.

The lynx eyes glinted to indicate Tariq's mood had swung. No longer incensed, yet to Alyssa he seemed infinitely more dangerous.

'Oh no, my beautiful slave girl,' he said softly. 'Don't imagine you'll be allowed to go scot free. You may have explained, but do you realise the hell you've put me through today?'

His grip on her wrists, high above her head, tightened and he shifted until she felt the press of

his body against hers. The situation was getting
out of hand. It was difficult to breathe, to think
straight. Alyssa closed her eyes hoping to clear
her senses, but the physical awareness of him was
too much. She struggled once more in a vain
attempt to loosen his grasp, but he kept her
fettered with arrogant ease. On balance, keeping
still was wiser. Wriggling against Tariq was
making her blood vessels dilate alarmingly.

'I haven't put you through anything,' she
protested, ordering her voice to remain level.

'What about my neat little dilemma?' he shot
back. 'Was it my duty to report you and those
other foolish women to the authorities, or did I
conveniently forget what I'd seen and make a
mockery of the laws of Ras-Al-Khan?' When she
squirmed for freedom, Tariq gave her a fierce
glare. 'Have you any idea how much you're
arousing me?' he demanded.

'Yes, I have!' she retorted, cursing chemistry.
With her arms manacled to the wall above her
head, the squirming had become the sensual glide
of female curves against an unrelenting male. She
could feel his arousal and knew her body was in
sympathy. 'So let me go!'

'Why should I? You've given me pain, worry,
anxiety. Won't justice be done if you recompense
me?'

'How?'

He bent to her. 'Like this,' he groaned, as if the
words were being forced from him. 'Like this.'

A bolt of something akin to electricity rocked
through her for his kiss was lovingly brutal, full
of hungry warmth. She felt the virile scrape of his

moustache as he persuaded her lips to part. After almost a year of widowhood, Alyssa was so rawly sensitised that his exploration of her mouth had her trembling. His body was spare and hard, the rigid male lines of his pelvis thrusting against her, and had Tariq allowed her arms to lower, they would have twined instinctively around him. Instead he adjusted his grip, holding her two wrists in one large hand while the other slid downwards. His fingertips brushed her cheek, her throat, and down until they reached the proud swell of her breast.

'*Habibati*,' he sighed, smoothing his thumb across the swollen peak which had lifted the fine silk of her blouson top. 'I must feast on your beauty, suckle at your breast.'

Alyssa whimpered, not clear whether in agreement or protest for, as his mouth covered hers again, she was lost—lost in the ecstasy of lips clinging to lips, lost as his fingers now moved to her other breast, languorously moulding until she whimpered again, wanting him.

'Tariq,' she sighed.

'We will be naked together.' He was whispering urgently. 'We *must* be. I can't pretend any more. I tell myself I don't, but I do.' He was talking to himself, his mouth hot and avid on her throat. 'It won't be easy, but——' He broke off, stepping back to release her wrists in a wrenching movement. Eyes glazed, he stretched out a hand to touch her hair, still curled loosely around her shoulders after the morning's modelling. 'So fair, so beautiful,' he murmured. His fingers slid among the ashen tresses until his grip tightened and he was cupping her head, pulling her back into his arms. 'Wear your hair free when you lie naked with me,' he implored.

'No, I won't. I mean, I'm not going to. We can't!' she sobbed and pushed frantically at his chest. 'This is madness, Tariq, you know it is. You order me to your office and now you——' She glanced wildly around. 'You speak of us being together but we both know it's wrong, it's impossible.'

'Not here.' He made a vague attempt to tame his rumpled hair. 'You don't imagine I would risk making love to you here, in my brother's house?' He gave a dry laugh and stood back, one-handedly tucking his tie into his jacket. 'Though we would not be disturbed. I instructed my servant that we were not to be interrupted, and *he* obeys the rules.' He stood for a moment, allowing his breathing to become calmer. 'Why is it I have this perverse inclination to . . . to *bed* you?'

Now that he was no longer so close, Alyssa retrieved some common sense.

'But I don't want to be bedded,' she said sharply.

'Then you won't be.'

'*Thank you.*'

They stood and glared at each other like two peevish children. The let-down was numbing. A minute ago they had been entwined, climbing the heights, but now he had kicked her down into the valley. Alyssa felt small and cheap and guilt-ridden, and it was all his fault. He should have known better than to take her in his arms, say all those words which had erotic images floating in her head. Her legs threatened to buckle, but she grabbed up her shoulder-bag, found a comb and began tidying her hair with breakneck speed. No doubt about it, she had risen far too early that morning. Or was Tariq wholly responsible for making her feel as if she had just staggered from the saddle of a bucking bronco? What had happened made no sense. The last time they had met at the radio station he had been the inscrutable overlord offering steeled responses, a foreigner in his robes, but now . . .

Tariq moved behind his desk, standing with hands spread, fingertips lightly touching the polished surface. 'I'd be grateful if you wouldn't model a second time. You already receive a handsome salary for your radio work so it's not as if you need extra money. Maybe this morning was done purely for kicks, but even so——'

'Is that an order?' Alyssa tossed the ashen curtain of hair from her shoulders. 'I was modelling in my spare time, and I doubt I'm the stuff of which centre-folds are made.'

'Aren't you?' His mouth curved. 'Don't sell yourself short, my beautiful slave girl.'

Indignation pricked. 'I'm not your slave girl.'

'No?' He shrugged, then continued, 'I'd prefer it if you wouldn't take on extra commitments. Moonlighting's bound to jeopardise your efficiency at the radio station.'

'I don't see why,' she began, only to clam up when she recalled how she had fallen asleep at the desk.

'I don't wish you to model.' Tariq's voice took on a cutting edge. 'You are not to exhibit yourself, either fully clothed or half naked. Modelling is not a fitting occupation for the person responsible for reading the world news. You weaken your position. You can't expect to be taken seriously if you're also a sex symbol.'

'The public would never connect a girl in a fashion photograph with a voice over the radio,' she protested, arguing for arguing's sake.

A jaw muscle tightened. 'In Ras-Al-Khan information—gossip—has a habit of spreading like wildfire, so please do as I ask. If you persist in this rebellion I shall——'

'Shall what?' Alyssa demanded, carried away by her smouldering contrariness. 'Punish me again? That's a delightful double standard. You object to me being a public sex symbol, yet you'd be delighted to have me as a private one. What's the matter, doesn't your fiancée look as good as I do in a swimming costume?'

She had gone too far, she knew she had. Dark eyes burning like coals, Tariq slammed his fist down on the desk. Whatever punishment followed this time, it would not be loving. Any hands he laid on her would not caress, they were more likely to strangle. The clatter of the telex machine saved her, for it sprang to life, printing out a screed and distracting them both. During the time the machine took to give its message, Tariq visibly brought himself to heel.

'I have no idea what Shamsa looks like in a swimsuit,' he said. 'She's constantly chaperoned, as befits the status of a sixteen-year-old sheikha.'

'She's only sixteen?' Alyssa could not prevent her surprise from showing.

'Sixteen and biddable. She will do as I tell her. *She* won't argue.'

Her chin jutted at the inference. 'And that's what you want?'

'No,' he said, looking down at his hands.

'Then why?' The two simple words covered a whole range of questions.

Tariq gave a sharp laugh. 'There are many considerations. I have responsibilities towards Ras-Al-Khan, towards my grandfather. I don't wish to disappoint him. He has suffered enough disappointments already.' He gestured towards the door. 'The car will be waiting to take you back to the station. I believe you must be there to read the news bulletin at ten?' She nodded. 'In that case you had better go. Good night.'

It was another blatant dismissal.

CHAPTER SIX

Now that she had known the ecstasy of his kiss, felt the drugging caress of his hands, Alyssa found it impossible to ban Tariq from her mind. Her feelings were ambivalent, vacillating from one extreme to the other in the time it took to draw breath. How she wished she could fling him out of her thoughts and out of her life forever. She hated the way he blew hot and cold. Hated the power he had over her. She hated *him*. No, she liked him—she never ever dared think about love.

After the incident at the coast palace, Tariq made sure they were never alone. Now most of their contact was by telephone, and when they did meet it was always in the presence of others. Sensible man, she thought wryly. Yet was he so sensible in other ways? Would a sensible man go into a marriage for reasons other than love?

The opportunity to find out presented itself when Alyssa spent a morning with Abdullah. A smiling youth with big dark eyes and a wispy beard of which he was inordinately proud, he proved to be both a willing interpreter and a charmer. They hit it off from the start. Patiently he took her along the waterfront, cajoling the *nakhodas*, the masters of the fishing boats, to take time off from their labours and talk.

'Cool drinks and air-conditioning now,' he

decreed, the moment she reached the end of her questioning. He was all for piling back into his Land-Cruiser and driving back to the city.

'Can't we stay here?' she pleaded, and because Abdullah admired her blonde hair he agreed to suffer the sun.

With a resigned sigh, he led her across the sand to a shabby open-air snack bar, grandly named the Hotel Qurayyah, installing her on a rickety bench beneath the shade of an *attap* canopy.

'I'm to be married next year,' he announced, when they had taken refreshing draughts of Seven-Up. 'To Fatima.'

'Congratulations.' Alyssa was not an expert at investigative interviews for nothing. 'You don't mind that your families have arranged the marriage.'

Raised eyebrows showed he considered her naïve. 'Why should I?'

'You wouldn't rather have chosen a wife yourself?' she suggested.

Abdullah laughed. 'But my family know exactly the kind of girl who'll be good for me. I would never find anyone more suitable myself. Fatima's parents and mine are close, and we have much in common. She's a clever girl, full of fun. She's been instructed in the skills of running a household and how to look after a man, so she'll make me a good wife.' He rubbed the black fuzz of his beard. 'Why would I choose a stranger?'

'Love?' she suggested tentatively.

'Ah, you mean sexual desire?'

'Yes.' The young man's outspokenness made her suppress a grin. 'That's a part of love.'

'Only a part. When I marry, I marry for life.'
Tipping the circular black *agal* forward so that it
balanced on his head at a rakish angle, Abdullah
became a sombre cherub. 'Sex will be important
to us, but also there is respect, affection and
companionship to consider. Love comes in many
different guises.' Alyssa nodded, surprised by his
maturity, but then she remembered her own
marriage and frowned. Each time she remembered, she seemed to bleed some more.
'Marriages in the Gulf are successful,' the young
man continued. 'Our divorce rate is minimal.
Because our marriages are rooted in com-
monsense, they are strong and stable and so our
children are raised in a secure environment.
There are few broken homes. We have our
priorities right.'

'And do you intend to take more than one
wife?'

He chuckled. 'It is written that each wife must
be treated equally. Supporting one woman is an
expensive business, two would be impossible!
Contrary to what you infidels believe, rarely do
Muslims take second wives these days.'

'I'm an infidel?' she teased, her blue eyes
sparkling.

'You,' he grinned. 'And Tariq.'

'Tariq?'

'He has yet to adopt the faith of Islam, and he
cannot wed Shamsa until he becomes a believer,
so . . .' Hands spread wide, Abdullah shrugged.

'So—what?'

'So time drags on and he remains a bachelor.
He hasn't even given instructions for a house to

be built for himself and his bride. Sheikh Suroor
is becoming very—what is it—uptight? For years
he has tried to marry off his daughters to Tariq.
First Rafiah, the eldest, was offered and then the
second girl and the third. Shamsa is his fourth
and final attempt. If Tariq wriggles out of
this ...' He dissolved into gales of laughter,
startling some nearby goats who froze before
timidly resuming their nibbles.

'Is he likely to wriggle out?' Alyssa asked.

'Not this time.' With a conscious effort,
Abdullah sobered. 'Before he lived abroad and
there were other influences, but now that he's
resident in Ras-Al-Khan he won't be able to
escape. Not that I believe he intends to.'

'Is Shamsa pretty?' she asked, telling herself
she was not really interested.

'The pick of the litter. She has long dark hair,
though it's not as long as my Fatima's hair.
Shamsa will make a devoted wife. She idolises
Tariq.'

'But why is Sheikh Suroor so determined to
have him as a son-in-law?'

'Because Tariq is destined to play a leading
role in Ras-Al-Khan's future. Our Petroleum
Minister is soon to retire, and it's strongly
rumoured that Tariq will be appointed. In that
position he'll have a lot of—clout?' He looked to
her for confirmation. 'Tariq's had to work hard
to overcome the taint of his foreign blood, but
now he's highly respected. He'll go far.'

'Does his foreign blood matter? I mean, surely
Sheikh Karim has foreign blood also?'

'Indeed not, Karim is pure Arab!' The young

man was indignant. 'Tariq is only a half-brother. He may rise to the top in the government, but he could never become ruler of Ras-Al-Khan, not with an infidel's blood in his veins.' He suddenly reddened, remembering he was speaking to an infidel. 'Not that the blood is bad but his father, Sheikh Hamed, did cut across our customs by marrying a white woman.'

'Sheikh Hamed had two wives?' Alyssa asked, finding endless fascination in this background information.

'Yes, but not at the same time.' Snapping his fingers, her escort conjured up fresh drinks and settled down to tell the tale. 'Hamed was first married in his teens to a sheikha from a neighbouring Gulf state. She died giving birth to Karim, who was raised as a Muslim and educated here.' The young man paused, enjoying her rapt attention. 'When Sheikh Hamed reached his late twenties, he committed a grievous sin. He travelled to England and acquired wife number two—the infidel.'

'Why did he go to England?'

'Because he was interested in horses, and when the oil money started to come in it was his ambition to acquire some of the best bloodstock available for Ras-Al-Khan.' He puffed out his chest. 'We Arabs *know* horses. However, over there he met an English woman, the daughter of a trainer, and foolishly Hamed fell in love. His father, our Ruler, wouldn't have cared if he had taken the woman as a mistress, but he said he wanted to marry her. His father was furious! He pleaded and cursed, used all manner of means to get him to change his mind, but it was one stubborn man meeting another. For a leading Arab to marry someone outside the faith was unthinkable so, in exchanging vows with the English woman, Hamed alienated himself from his family and his country. There was so much bitterness that he swore he'd never set foot on the soil of Ras-Al-Khan again. Nowadays people are more broadminded and a mixed marriage would be acceptable, but back then ...' Abdullah gestured to indicate the foibles of those who had lived in the Dark Ages.

'Yet Tariq's been handling this country's oil interests for a number of years?'

The young man nodded. 'Although Hamed didn't return, he had no wish for his son to be robbed of his birthright. Sheikh Ahmad, Tariq's grandfather, was also eager he should play a part in the development of Ras-Al-Khan. When he was a boy, mediators were despatched and eventually it was agreed Tariq would be accepted into the Al Zahini fold, despite his father disgracing the name. Hamed was hesitant about Tariq settling here—pride, I suppose.' He wrinkled his nose. 'But Hamed's death six months ago removed the final obstacles. Apparently Tariq's mother is content for him to devote his life to Ras-Al-Khan. I think she understands how, by adopting the faith and marrying Shamsa, Tariq is absolving his father's sins. He's redeeming his honour, and honour is important among us Arabs.' Abdullah stretched his arms above his head. 'But the marriage arrangements are moving so slowly. Tariq

questions many things. My father says——' He
thought better of telling her what his father had
said and tossed a few silver coins on to the table.
'Shall we go?'

'So when is Tariq likely to be married?' Alyssa
asked, walking beside him across the burning
sand.

The young man shrugged. '*Inshallah*,' he said.

Understanding Tariq's motivation did not mean
Alyssa agreed with the path he had chosen to
take. But his decisions were nothing to do with
her. She couldn't interfere. Not that she wanted
to, yet in the weeks which led down to the
completion of his remit she nursed a vague need
to put her hand on his arm and enquire if he
really was doing the right thing? What would his
reaction have been? Probably she would have
been told, in no uncertain terms, to mind her own
business.

And now Tariq had gone. He had cleared his
files from the boardroom table, leaving Mr
Harding working out his notice and Mohammed
Nasser in charge. Oil matters had claimed him.
But before he had departed, the staff had been
assembled to hear what had been accomplished
and what the sheikh expected them to accomplish.
One particular sentence had delighted her. In
passing, he had said, 'Mrs Brett's skills are of
great value to Radio Ras-Al-Khan.' Alyssa smiled
as she filled a paper cup with coffee and carried it
across the presenters' lounge. Now it seemed as
sure as death and taxes that a further contract
would be offered her in eighteen months' time.

As sure as death. The phrase brought a shiver.
She sat down, thrown back to her life with
Douglas, understanding *his* motivation. Poor
Douglas. With a sigh, Alyssa sipped her coffee
and slowly began to review the past.

A bride of six months, it had taken a chance
visit to the hospital where she had taken her first
radio steps to explain Doug's increasingly
worrying behaviour. She had been striding along
in search of a friend who ran the patients' record
request programme, when a corner had been
rounded and she had cannoned into the surgeon
who had operated on her husband a year before
their marriage. She didn't know Mr Menzies
well, but remembered him from the days when
the record programme had been in her care.

After the usual greetings, the surgeon had
looked stern. 'You must make certain Douglas
comes in for his regular check-up. He missed the
last one, and he's in too bad a shape to get away
with that kind of irresponsibility.'

'What check-up?' she had asked. The operation
eighteen months ago—for a heart defect—had
been completely successful, or so Douglas had
always vowed. 'I thought everything was . . .
fine?'

'Good God, no!' Mr Menzies eyes had
narrowed. 'You mean you don't . . . You mean,
he hasn't . . .' He grasped her arm. 'Oh, my poor
dear, come along to my room.' There he had
peered at her over his bi-focals. 'I can't make this
easy, but you're a sensible type. Which is more
than can be said of your husband,' he added,
using the voice of doom. 'All I can do is tell you

what Douglas should have told you long before you agreed to marry him. That the surgery he underwent was to no effect, that the problem with his heart proved to be inoperable.'

Shock and mind-shattering confusion had half lifted her from the chair. 'But—but he doesn't seem ill,' she had stuttered. 'He is a little pale at times, I admit, and edgy, but I thought that was because he's working long hours. He's setting up a new business and——'

Mr Menzies had shaken a finger. 'Long hours are out. It's essential your husband avoids stress, whether overtiring himself physically or becoming emotionally wound up.' He moved his hand again, now smoothing across an invisible plateau. 'Level pegging is vital. No ups, no downs. No harsh words, no fights. At least, not if he wants to stretch out his time.'

'His time?' Alyssa had shuddered. 'How long is his time?'

'If he carries on like he's doing now—no check-ups, no self-help—I'd give him twelve months.'

She had felt faint. 'Only twelve months?'

'Longer if he learns to live at peace.'

'How much longer?'

The surgeon had shrugged. 'Two years, maybe three.'

'And Doug's aware of this—time limit?' Alyssa asked, trying hard to assimilate what she was being told.

'Yes. He tackled me straight after the operation, insisted on knowing the worst.'

'And you told him?' Her despair and bewilderment abruptly metamorphosed into body-shaking anger. 'But that was downright cruel! Doug's insecure at the best of times. He's not the type who could cope with a death sentence hanging over his head. No wonder he's going to pieces.'

'Is he? Shall I prescribe some tablets?'

'No. And he isn't. Or maybe he is. I don't know.' She had hardly been able to see the surgeon through the blur of scalding tears. 'I'm going home. I'm going to talk to Doug.'

But she *had* known her young husband was going to pieces, known it for a long time. As Alyssa had trudged back through the rain she had finally faced up to the fact that Doug's behaviour had always been suspect, no matter how many excuses she had made for him. Now she understood the tantrums, the violent swings of moods. He was living with a grim secret, living in constant hell. As Mr Menzies had said, there was no easy way to talk about the subject, so that evening she had told Doug, as calmly as she could, what she had learned. She did not ask why he hadn't told her, it was too late for that. He needed her love and support, not her reproaches.

'I've thought everything through, Doug,' she had explained. 'You can sell the bus company and we'll manage on my salary. That'll give you the chance to slow down and take things easy.' She had been sitting on the arm of his chair, a hand resting on his shoulder, but he had flung her from him. He had jumped to his feet and glared at her, a slender young man with fevered grey eyes and a pinched expression.

'I don't want your damn money,' he had spat. 'And I don't want your pity.'

'It's not pity, it's love!' she had protested.

'Never! You only married me because you felt sorry for me.'

'That's not true! And how could I? I didn't know then that——' The words had been trapped in her throat, but Doug had appeared to relish saying them for her.

'That I'm going to die? Maybe not, but in your eyes I've always been a lost little boy and you're a natural comforter, aren't you, Lyss?' he had jeered. 'Well, I can manage fine without your pity. And as far as selling the company goes, forget it! You always have thought I'm a rotten businessman. Yes, you have,' he had insisted. 'Now you're using this as an excuse to sabotage my success. But I'll show you. I'll be a success despite *you*! And despite that snake-tongued mother of yours, and all the other people who are forever telling me I'm like a bloody bull at a bloody gate.'

'Calm down,' she had implored, terrified to see his colour draining. 'Continue the business if you must, but at least cut down on hours. Mr Menzies insists you go for regular check-ups and——'

'And I insist you stop bloody interfering,' Doug had yelled, hands trembling with fury.

'I only want to help. *Please*.'

'Okay.' He had pushed his hands into his pockets and marched jerkily back and forth. 'You can help by keeping your mouth shut. You're not to tell anyone—not darling sister Meg, not a

single living soul, about my bad heart. I've had it
with pity. I don't want anyone feeling sorry
because I'm a loser. We just go on as we are. We
don't let anyone in on the secret.' Douglas had
grabbed a Bible from the bookshelf. 'Swear on
this,' he had demanded. 'Swear you'll never
betray me.'

Not knowing what else to do, Alyssa had
sworn, then suddenly Doug had collapsed on his
knees in front of her and sobbed in her arms like
a baby. Tears streaming down his face, he had
apologised for shouting, said he loved her, he
needed her, and promised that now the air had
been cleared everything would improve. But the
very next day he had gone back on his word. He
had declared his health and life expectancy to be
forbidden topics, and had walked out of the
house when she protested.

Alyssa crumpled the paper cup in her fist.
Having known what went on inside Doug's head
had not helped at all. Her understanding of
Tariq's psyche was equally pointless. Like Doug
he would go on his own way, though unlike Doug
he was eminently capable of transforming a sticky
situation into triumph. Shamsa sounded to be
already in love with him, and faced with a young
and pretty bride, eager to please, who knew but
that Tariq would rapidly fall in love with her
once they were sharing the same bed?

Forget Tariq, she groaned. You won't be
coming into contact again. Just now he's in the
States bringing some oil deal to fruition, and once
he returns the marriage wheels must surely start

to turn. *Inshallah* does not mean, 'It may happen and it may not', it means, 'It *will* happen when Allah decrees'.

She collected a fresh cup of steaming coffee. Ends were tying up nicely. At long last Brough's manuscript had been finished to his satisfaction, and though he reported that the second saga was gestating Alyssa had asked him to find another typist. With her place on the radio team secure, she was taking no chances. Moonlighting, in any way, shape or form, was taboo.

Yesterday Lennie had argued hard and long to plead the modelling case. 'Byron reckons you're dynamite. You've seen the photographs, so you know they're superb. The brochure will be a knock-out. Why about-turn and decide you don't intend to model again? The money's good, and you want money.'

'I don't have time,' she had said firmly, tired of an argument which had meandered on far too long.

A thought had scampered into Lennie's head and bitten him. 'It's that scare at the harbour! You don't want to model swimwear again?' he had prodded. 'No big deal. Byron's promised to keep ultra respectable in future. And don't worry about whoever watched, he's never spilled any beans. In fact, I bet he's got himself a hernia with driving around the city from morning until night, hoping to grab a repeat performance.'

'I doubt it,' she had said drily. No one had been told of Tariq's reprimand. There seemed little point when his rage had been directed solely at *her*.

'I used to think you were a woman with spunk,' Lennie had sulked. 'But at heart you're a prude.'

Some prude! Try as she might, Alyssa could not stop from reliving time and time again the minutes when she had been imprisoned against the office wall by the barricade of Tariq's body. His slave girl, he had called her, and how right he had been. One kiss, one caress, and she would have willingly followed him to the ends of the earth. Her pulse vibrated. If he had chosen to make love to her, there and then on the carpet, her resistance would have been a paltry thing. Alyssa balled her fists. She despised him for making her so compliant but, worst of all, she despised herself.

She projected forward her current saving rate. Nigel Dutton would be paid off in full in two-and-a-half years. For a moment she indulged in the heady joy of how it would feel when his control over her life had been lifted. She would soar free as a bird! She would go where she wanted, and do whatever she wished. But it was not as simple as that. The fear came in a sharp wave. Nigel Dutton had trapped her in a net, he would never let her wriggle free. There had been no mention of him in Meg's latest letter, but did no news mean good news? Doubtful. Maybe his unblinking crocodile eyes had fastened on an alternative prey. Again doubtful. His appetite for young ladies was well known. As far as he was concerned, the more the merrier. Yet maybe he would relent if she established her goodwill by feeding the monthly payments?

Enough of this introspection, she commanded herself. Alyssa was reaching for cuttings on pearl diving, the basis of a future programme, when the 'phone rang. Mohammed Nasser was on the line, requesting her presence. On her arrival in his office, he spent several minutes praising her fishing programme which had gone out a day or two earlier, then gave an apologetic smile.

'What I really wanted to see you about is to ask a favour.'

'Shoot,' she said flippantly.

'Well, Diva's down with measles, of all things, and Susan went off on leave last week, hiking through the Himalayan foothills.'

'Diva and Susan from the television service?' she confirmed, not quite sure where all this was leading.

'Yes. And Clare rang ten minutes' ago to say her little boy's been involved in a road accident. Nothing serious, but she's stuck at the emergency department with him. So ...' Mohammed paused. 'So I'd be grateful if you'd fill in, just for this evening.' He reached for a folder she recognised as her personnel file, and leafed through. 'You've done schools' television in the UK, so this'll be a cinch.'

'Suppose I freeze or have hysterics?' Alyssa wondered out loud. 'Cinch' was overly optimistic. The anonymity of the microphone held no fears, but to appear on a screen where every fault was magnified to disaster level! 'And the schools' television was only for six weeks,' she pointed out.

'You can cope. The news consists mainly of

film clips with voice-overs. After a crash course you'll be fine. It's a great opportunity to widen your scope.'

'Couldn't Brough widen his scope?' she suggested.

Mohammed shook his head. 'The television news is always read by a young lady, so the viewers expect continuity. Please help.' He grinned at her. 'You're always so cool and composed.'

'Flatterer!'

'Then you'll do it?'

She gave a wry smile. 'I suppose so.'

Yes, both loop earrings were in place, unlikely to come adrift and clatter to the desk during the next thirty minutes. Yes, the cowl neckline of her oyster silk dress lay even beneath her fidgeting fingers. Alyssa coughed, smoothed a hand to check her hair remained twisted into the svelte chignon, took a sip of water and coughed again. Hypertension and complete amnesia had set in. Two minutes before transmission and her mind was a blank. Between her ears sat solid concrete. Nothing remained from the crash course, even the sentences on the sheets of papers before her appeared to have been written in Swahili. When she opened her mouth to rehearse the first line, a croak emerged. How did punctuation and pronunciation stand a chance when mere speech was beyond her? A five-year-old fresh from kindergarten could do better. She coughed and cleared her throat again.

'Ten seconds to go. Roll VTR. Five seconds to

go,' a dismembered voice announced. 'Evening News logo is on screen. Ten seconds to in vision. Announcer five-four-three-two-one, you are in vision.'

The camera eye winked obscenely and Alyssa shot it a bright unsteady smile.

'Good evening, this is the news. And first, the headlines,' she began and, as if like magic, her professional's spine of steel snapped erect. Intent on reading the script in intelligible English, she forgot her fear of sneezing, or being reduced to hiccups, or what she would do if a fly chose to land on her nose. When the first filmed report came in on cue, Alyssa relaxed a fraction. So far, so good. Take it calmly, girl. She congratulated herself on getting her tongue around the names of a visiting Thai delegation, and on keeping a straight face when some minor official appeared to be named Mr Mecan Suckthistle. Everyone, from news director to vision mixer, was rooting for her, indeed the death sentence had been threatened if technical faults marred the programme.

'And from the news team and myself, Alyssa Brett, good night,' she concluded, thirty minutes later, her farewell smile more dazzling than the Milky Way.

As the camera light snapped off, Alyssa crumpled. Nervous tension had kept her bolt upright for the past half hour, but now there was a distinct danger she might slide off the chair and collapse in a heap. Her legs were jellied, her heart pumping madly. She wanted to laugh and cry, both at the same time. No serious gaffes had been made, had they? She had said the correct words in the correct order?

Someone clapped her on the back. 'Good girl.'

The video machine operator appeared. 'Wasn't too nerve-racking, was it?'

'Oh no!' she replied breathlessly, and was amazed when her sarcasm went unnoticed. Smiles and praise came from all sides.

'How did it feel to be star for a night?' teased the news director, a chubby pleasant-faced young man from Illinois.

Alyssa gabbled off into a long involved explanation of how reading the television news was fifty times worse than going to the dentist.

'Something akin to the Spanish Inquisition,' she was exclaiming, when one of the newsroom girls waved from the studio door.

'Telephone, urgent. For Alyssa.'

The news director pointed her in the right direction. 'Get cracking, honey. Could be Mohammed on the line with his congratulations, or maybe Cubby Broccoli offering you the female lead in the next James Bond movie!'

She floated to the telephone.

'Alyssa Brett speaking.'

'Good evening, ma'am. This is His Excellency Sheikh Tariq's secretary speaking. My master would like a word with you.'

She had been loose-limbed and sprawly with relief that her newscasting debut had gone so smoothly, but this mention of Tariq promptly tightened her up. Yet why would Tariq call her from the States? Was this some kind of international link-up?

'Put him through,' she said, after a pause.

'He wishes to speak to you in person. A car has been despatched which should reach the television complex in ten minutes' time.'

'You mean he's in Ras-Al-Khan?' She knew she sounded dense.

'His Excellency returned from abroad yesterday. The driver has been ordered to collect you from the main entrance. You will be there.'

Was that a question or an order? Alyssa was still wondering how to reply when the line went dead.

CHAPTER SEVEN

'Is Mohammed putting your name forward for an OBE?' teased the news director, coming in as she jettisoned the 'phone.

Alyssa tugged at an earring. 'No, that was a summons from Tariq. I'm supposed to go and see him this evening.'

'This evening? Wow, you must have knocked him out cold with your performance, honey. Maybe he intends to give you the freedom of Ras-Al-Khan!'

'I'm not going.' She folded her arms and glared. How could she cope with a summons from Tariq while her nerves were still jangling? She couldn't handle his stiff formality, or his lovemaking, or whatever it was he proposed to throw at her this time. Her watch said almost eleven, and what right had he to demand her presence at this hour? Nothing in her contract stipulated she was on call any time night or day. 'No, I'm not going,' she repeated, furious because she felt so alarmed.

'I think you should. Look, you're bound to get red-carpet treatment. His Excellency will congratulate you on a fine performance and you'll be safely back home come midnight.' The news director tapped the side of his head with two fingers. 'Pays to be political, kid. Why clash with the powers that be? Why screw things up by being plain contrary?'

She stopped to consider his argument. Tariq would never fire her merely because she failed to keep one appointment, but whichever way you looked at it, her immediate future did rest in his hands. Keeping the money rolling in was vital, so why cause unnecessary trouble? Alyssa sighed, rebellion collapsing.

'Okay, I'll go.'

'That's a smart girl. Now trot off to make-up and have them remove the goo.' The young man surveyed the eyelids which had been painted with shimmering colour, the high cheekbones where blusher made a dramatic impact. 'On the other hand, you could stick with the warpaint and have a shot at enticing Tariq away from his betrothed.'

She twitched her nose. 'No, thank you.'

Wearing only a trace of eye shadow and mascara, Alyssa crossed the forecourt. The driver beside the Mercedes was a different one from last time, and she was relieved when he made no attempt to talk. Drained from the excess of nervous energy used up during the past few hours, she wanted nothing more than to sit quietly. She leant back against the soft leather upholstery as the car moved off, and allowed her mind to drift for, assuming Tariq had approved of her newscasting—and surely he must?—she had nothing to worry about.

How would Doug have reacted to her television performance? Would he have been pleased? The honest answer was *no*. Publicly proud, at heart he had resented her career, her mild celebrity, her glowing health and strength. She could not blame him. His emotions, like the emotions of anyone trapped in his situation, had been distorted. She closed her eyes. Oh Doug! If only you would have let me help. If only we could have faced your dilemma together. If only . . .

Once again turbanned guards leapt to open the gates, and once again the Mercedes purred through the gardens, though now all she could see were the fountains, silver plumes of water a stark contrast against the velvet black of the night. The car stopped beneath the portico and Alyssa stepped out, turning as a white-robed figure came from the palace. Half smiling, she prepared to greet the manservant she had expected and was thrown off balance when she discovered Tariq had come to meet her himself.

'Good evening, Mrs Brett.'

'Good evening.' Her insides were marshmallow. During his absence she had managed to convince herself she was glad their contact was over, but here she was, ecstatic yet fearful of being in his company again. Analysis of her emotional responses was beyond her, but suddenly she was desperate for his approval. 'Did you see me on television this evening, reading the news?' she asked eagerly.

Tariq waited until the Mercedes had begun to draw away and then said, 'I did. It's been quite a day for you, hasn't it?'

Alarm bells rang. His voice was ice cold, and was it imagination or did the glitter of his eyes indicate contained violence? Whatever his reason for requiring her presence, he was not an admirer about to hand out bouquets. Tonight a head would be on a platter—hers! But she was in no fit state to defend herself, emotionally or otherwise.

'Yes, it has been,' Alyssa agreed, smoothing a wayward ash-blonde wisp from her brow. 'Would you mind if we talked tomorrow? Right now I'm too exhausted to——'

'*Ta'ala!*' he commanded, spinning on his heel.

Resenting him like mad, there seemed no option but to follow him through the heavy doors. Across the marble hall and out on to a moon-dappled courtyard they went, and he never once looked back. Bobbing in his wake like a dinghy tied to an ocean liner, Alyssa's temper flared. How dare he treat her like this—like a slave girl? Slave girl! Her mind exploded, for the term held too many dangerous connotations. White headdress billowing, the black ropes of the *agal* streaming down his back, Tariq strode across the courtyard and down the silent corridors, taking her pursuit for granted. Alyssa found herself having to almost run in order to keep up, and by the time they reached his office, she was pink-cheeked and out of breath.

'Didn't you think my performance was okay, for a first time?' she panted, before he could speak. 'Everyone at the studios approved.'

Tariq had reached his desk, standing behind it with shoulders at military precision. 'They would, you shone.'

She shone! His praise, even though snapped out, made her go limp. She had needed his praise so much, and now he *had* praised her.

'Thank you,' she said, smiling like a fool.

'As you also shone in today's edition of the

Ras-Al-Khan Times. I must applaud your timing.'

'The *Ras-Al-Khan Times*? What do you mean?'

Now she noticed a newspaper on his desk. Tariq grabbed it and strode forward, brandishing it beneath her nose.

'I mean how you thrilled everyone at breakfast by appearing as the teasing minx, and this evening switched to holier-than-thou newsreader. What a contrast—mistress and wife rolled into one, every man's fantasy!' he jeered.

Alyssa was totally confused. She hadn't seen the paper today. 'What are you talking about?'

'I can provide other descriptions which are far less polite. I asked you not to model again, but you do. And now this!' He thrust the newspaper at her. 'What is it with you—a lust for the limelight?'

Her eyes flew to the half-page advertisement. There she was in the one-piece maillot stretched out horizontally, breasts tip-tilted, one leg bent at the knee. She was involved in a love affair with the camera, an alluring curve to her mouth, and obviously lost in a world of her own.

'I'm wearing a respectable bathing suit. The advertisement must have passed the censors, so nobody's going to be offended.' After surviving a traumatic evening at the television studios, Alyssa was damned if she would tolerate this victimisation, for victimisation was what it was. She discovered an emergency high-octane mixture of defiance. 'And I haven't modelled a second time. I obeyed your command. This photograph was taken on the *dhow*. Byron took hundreds.'

Tariq snapped his fingers against the news-paper. 'Including provocative ones like this?'

'I didn't knowingly pose to be provocative. It just happened.'

A sardonic brow arched. 'Just happened? Like it just happened that you filled the television news slot on the very same day that the advertisement appears?'

'I had no prior knowledge that I'd be asked to be on television. I was helping out in an emergency,' Alyssa informed him, packing her words in ice. 'I was also unaware that this advertisement was scheduled. I understood the photographs were destined for a brochure, and that was all. I apologise if——'

'Apologise!' He snatched his *kaffia* from his head and tossed it on to the desk, leaving himself free to run both hands through his thick dark hair. 'Can't you see what's happened? In one stroke you've reduced the credibility of the television news service to zero.'

'No, I haven't!'

'All right.' He took a deep steadying breath. 'All right, maybe not to zero, but you've certainly damaged our confidence rating. How can the news appear sober and convincing if it's presented by a woman who was blazoned across the morning papers like some Lorelei? There's such a thing as horses for courses, and in an Islamic society in particular, it's important for the newsreader to be modest, demure and dependable, but you——'

His anger boiled over again, and Alyssa stood mute. She felt as if she was in the dead eye of a hurricane, too wrung out by the evening's events to care any more. Let him fume! Let him accuse! She hardly listened as his rage swirled around her.

'I feel just as strongly about Ras-Al-Khan's broadcasting services as you,' she said, when Tariq ran out of breath. 'I regret what's happened, but I still maintain you're over-reacting. The advertisement is perfectly ordinary, and as far as people connecting me in a bathing costume with me on television, that seems doubtful. In the photograph my hair's loose and tangled, half-covering my face, whereas tonight I appeared on screen with it caught back into a chignon. I looked quite different.'

He shot her a slanted glance. 'Maybe,' he admitted.

'*Definitely.*'

Her flat conviction seemed to drain him of fight. Tariq lifted the newspaper and studied the advertisement again.

'You could be right.'

'I am. The general public would never have made the link.'

'Perhaps I have over-reacted,' he mumbled. 'It's just that—it's just that when I saw the photograph this morning I wanted you so damned much!' Alyssa gazed at him in alarm. 'I looked at the curves of your body, imagined the feel of you, the fragrance of you and—and I assumed every other man must feel the same. They wouldn't, of course. They haven't held you in their arms.' He flipped the newspaper back on to the desk. 'Maybe only I saw the teasing minx.'

'But I don't tease,' she protested.

'Don't you? No, perhaps you don't, not consciously.'

Tariq slid a forefinger into his mouth and withdrew it, reaching forward to gently trace the glistening tip around the shape of her lips. The serious look in his eyes, the moist sensual stroke of his finger outlining so intimately, made her mouth water. He was going to kiss her, and she could feel the expectancy in her body—a tentative stillness, an ache.

Alyssa stepped back. 'I must go.'

'Yes,' he agreed, also stepping back. 'I understand your first radio documentary went down well. Has Mohammed raised the prospect of a second series?'

'He's asked me to sketch out six more,' she said, grateful he had switched to business.

'And you're happy about that?'

'Yes.' Her blue eyes danced. 'This part of the world is fascinating, and so far I've only skimmed the surface. I'm itching to learn more about the customs and the people.'

Tariq grinned. 'You're itching to learn more about me?'

'Not you,' she said warily. 'You're not typical.'

'I have a wide knowledge of the Gulf's culture,' he protested lightheartedly. 'When I was a boy I used to camp in the desert, sleep beneath the stars. I keep promising myself I'll become involved in that kind of activity again.' He sighed, suddenly thoughtful. 'But as you say, I'm not typical. At times Ras-Al-Khan and its ways appear as foreign to me as they must to you.

When you've grown up in the West it's difficult
not to relate to a Western lifestyle.' His glance
told her that maybe he regretted the admission.
'Don't get me wrong. I'm very close to my family
here, but as you can imagine there are frustra-
tions. So much is left to the whim of Allah! Still,
it's important I validate my place within the Al
Zahini fold. Becoming a Muslim and taking
Shamsa as my bride makes sense. Everyone's so
keen for me to do that, but occasionally I
wonder—well, I wonder if *I* want it, too.'

'You'd rather stay a bachelor?' Alyssa suggested.

'No. I *do* want to be married. I *do* want
children.' He seemed to be involved in a debate
with himself. 'I don't want to be alone. I want to
have a wife. I want to share.'

She frowned. 'So?'

'So nothing. Take no notice. It's just the
Western male in me getting fractious again. It'll
pass. When's your next free day?'

'Thursday, why?' she asked, puzzled by the
abrupt change of tack.

'On Thursday I'll drive you out to the Ali
Obaid oasis where Suroor has a half-finished
retreat, another of his follies,' Tariq said, with ill-
concealed scorn. 'He had this brainwave of
recreating the Hanging Gardens of Babylon in
the middle of the desert. It didn't come to
fruition, of course, but it's a useful bolt hole
when I feel an urge to be alone.' He paused. 'On
Thursday I'll be alone there—with you.'

The emotional current which zizzed between
them warned Alyssa that now was the time for

retreat, to turn tail and flee. Common sense told
her she should run pellmell from the sultry
corsair who was looking at her as if he wanted to
devour her whole, but she could not move. Tariq
took a step forward and enclosed her in his arms.
Instantly their mouths locked. They began
kissing in an intense, starving kind of way and
she clung to him, recharging her emotional
batteries from the urgency of his desire. Tariq
was strong and sure. He wanted to love her and
she wanted it, too. Drowning in the warmth of
his embrace, she sighed when his hands began to
move over her. She felt his fingers search for the
back zip of her dress.

'Darling, Tariq,' she murmured.

'No,' he said, and she heard the rough edge of
his breathing. He raised his head, his dark eyes
full of anguish. 'No, we can't. Not here, not
tonight, *habibati*. It would be too dangerous.' He
straightened, gripping her shoulders as if to
steady them both. 'We must be—sensible.' The
word came out with difficulty.

'I don't want to be sensible,' Alyssa whimpered.
'I want——'

'I know what you want,' he soothed, tenderly
stroking her hair. 'And I want it, too. But we
must be discreet.'

CHAPTER EIGHT

DISCREET! Alyssa had been too carried away by
the eagerness of his kisses to notice the word's
significance, but when she awoke next morning it
bombarded her senses with the harsh clarity of a
klaxon call. Discreet! She jerked from the pillow.
Free from the lingering pressure of his mouth,
the caress of his hands, their lovemaking took on
quite a different slant. She could read between
the lines. She was too worldly-wise not to know
Tariq's need for discretion meant one thing, and
only one thing—he intended they embark on a
furtive love affair.

The wealthy Arab and the blonde was a
cliché—a cliché which sickened her. Voicing his
so-called disquiet at taking Shamsa as his bride
had been a ploy, part of a softening-up process to
ensure she would be sympathetic, and how *very*
sympathetic she had been. God! she was a fool.
Alyssa took a deep breath, wondering what would
have happened if Tariq had failed to call a halt.
She shook her head in despair, She didn't need to
wonder, she *knew*.

'Until Thursday,' he had murmured, leading
her by the hand through the sleeping palace and
she, like the naïve creature she was, had made no
protest.

She leapt out of bed to search feverishly
through the telephone directory. Before seven it

might be, but the day started early in the Gulf and there was no time to waste. Ten minutes later she was almost screaming with frustration. A batch of numbers were listed for the coast palace, but several of the lines seemed continually engaged, while others had rung and rung, forcing her to abort. When she had received an answer, she'd either found herself connected with someone who didn't speak English or else had been asked to wait and had been abandoned, listening to sweet nothing. She was just about to give up hope when Tariq's secretary came on the line.

'Can I be of any assistance?' he enquired.

Alyssa breathed a sigh of relief. 'I'd like to speak with Sheikh Tariq, please.' Abruptly she felt uncomfortable, sure the man would be suspicious of such an early morning 'phone call. What role did he imagine she played in Tariq's life? He knew of her late-evening visit, so did he automatically assume she had become his master's lover? Had other women been driven to the coast palace in the Mercedes? True she had heard no rumours, but Tariq would have been discreet. *Discreet!* For all she knew he could have wenched with starlets in the West and now intended to continue a varied sex life in the Middle East, married or not. No, she hadn't heard any tales about him, but plenty circulated about other Arabian sheikhs. Was he really any different? 'I need to discuss a radio matter,' she added, hoping she would convey through her tone that her reputation was beyond reproach.

'I regret to advise that His Excellency left an

hour ago for an off-shore installation, ma'am. Would you care to leave a message?'

'Would you tell him Mrs Brett is unable to keep her Thursday appointment. Her *business* appointment.'

'I will.'

'You'll make certain he gets the message?' Alyssa needed to be positive there would be no slip up.

'Be assured, ma'am. I have taken a written note. His Excellency will be informed on his return.'

'Thank you.'

She rang off. Should she follow the 'phone call with a note, just to make sure Tariq understood? But writing to inform him that he had made a mistake and she was not the gullible blonde he had imagined, lacked dignity. How did you put down in black and white that you balked at becoming a man's mistress?

The whole day was fraught. Whenever the 'phone rang, whether in her apartment or at the broadcasting complex, Alyssa leapt into frozen apprehension, terrified Tariq might be on the line with an indignant rebuttal or another summons into his presence—a summons she was adamant would be ignored this time. But he did not get in touch. One day passed, followed by two more, and she recognised he had had second thoughts about starting a hole-in-the-corner affair. Tariq was no fool. His grandfather might turn a blind eye on a romance abroad, but he would never condone one in Ras-Al-Khan, not with Tariq poised to marry Shamsa. The heat of his desire may have prompted him to hint at a relationship, but common sense would have now prevailed. He would no more want a spurious affair than she.

On an even keel once more, Alyssa could devote her energy to her work. The second programme went out and received acclaim, the third was in the bag, the fourth required finishing touches, the fifth ... By the time Thursday loomed she was more than ready for a break. She slept late, an unaccustomed luxury, opening her eyes to a sun-filled room. Over breakfast she laid plans. Sunbathing and swimming in the Colonnade's pool this morning, while after lunch she'd catch up on long-overdue letters to friends back home.

She was pulling her bikini from the drawer when the door bell pealed a fanfare. Brough. When she had passed him in the corridor the previous evening she had reminded him, yet again, that the office typewriter continued to languish in her apartment. He must be keeping his promise and coming to collect it.

'Hold on.' Alyssa threw on a blue satin robe and padded across the lounge, but when she opened the door her welcoming smile faded. Tariq was standing there, a modern-day cowboy in plaid shirt and blue jeans. 'I've cancelled our trip,' she blabbed, her heart breaking all records for rapid acceleration. 'I rang your office a few days ago and your secretary promised he'd tell you. *He promised.*'

Her wail of distress made him grin. 'He did tell me, but surely you realise I rarely take no for an answer?' He glanced up and down the corridor. 'May I come in? Precious little happens in Ras-Al-Khan which escapes the attention of the Colonnade's inmates, but I'd feel happier if they didn't know about my visit. Especially as you greet me wearing so few clothes.'

Backing away, Alyssa tugged at her robe. Skin damp from a recent shower, the fine material clung to outline her figure in a way which had Tariq's eyes moving over her in undisguised interest. This morning he was light years away from the aloof Arabian overlord; in short-sleeved shirt and jeans he was just another man. Not *exactly* just another man, she admitted with a sinking heart. Alyssa was scared to meet his eyes. If she focused on the warmth of his look, on the curve of his mouth beneath the dark bristles of his moustache, she would be disarmed. No matter how much her traitorous body ached to be held close, she must follow the dictates of her head and chop down this sapling relationship before it had chance to put down roots.

'I'm sorry, Tariq, but I don't want to go out with you,' she announced, with bare feet set firmly apart.

'Yes, you do.'

She sighed. 'Maybe, but I'm not going to.'

'Why? Because you're frightened we might . . .' he scowled, '. . . might begin an affair?'

'That's right.' Her voice was faint. How could he see through her so easily? His mastery of her state of mind was dismaying.

'But an affair wouldn't suit me, either. The consequences could be frightening.' As if to emphasise the danger, Tariq aimed a forefinger at his temple and fired an imaginary gun. 'Do you think I'd put your reputation and mine at risk?'

'Well . . . no.'

'Then trust me.'

'But you know how unwise it would be for us to be seen together,' Alyssa persisted, ignoring the burning vitality of his look. 'You've said yourself how rumours circulate, how you shouldn't be alone with me.'

'Accepted, but you want to learn more about the life of the Gulf? Yes?' he insisted. She nodded tentatively. 'So, just for today we'll be platonic friends researching a radio programme. There's no harm in that. We'll be anonymous any way.'

'How? Everyone will recognise your car. Someone's probably drooling over it right now,' she added, with a touch of cynicism.

Tariq shook his head. 'I've borrowed Abdullah's Land-Cruiser. That has number plates so it'll be one of many.'

'People might recognise *you*.'

'Dressed like this I fade into the crowd.'

Alyssa doubted that very much. His inbuilt confidence and dark good looks guaranteed Tariq was the focus of attention anywhere.

'I'd still prefer——'

'*Imshi!*' Pure imperious prince, he pointed towards the bedroom door. 'Go and get ready. Any more rebellion and I'll have no alternative but to punish you.' He grinned mischievously. 'Don't overlook my sadistic streak.'

Five minutes later, Alyssa emerged in white

cotton pants, with a matching blazer over a
sleeveless black silk shirt. Her hair had been
knotted back with a length of black chiffon, and
she had pushed sunglasses on to the top of her
head. In her hand was a cheap straw safari helmet
she had haggled for in the *souk*.

To her relief they went down in the lift and
across the car park without meeting anyone she
knew, and once installed inside the Land-Cruiser
the fear of being spied faded. Initially they
followed the road which ran alongside the river,
and as Tariq pointed out places of interest and
explained their history, she began to relax. The
built-up area soon petered out into flat scrub
desert where blackened shrubs fought for survival,
and several miles later dunes took shape. They
were red-gold dunes, where not so much as a
footprint marred the rippled surface of the sand.

'I hope you know where we're going?' she
teased, when they had been motoring for quite a
while. 'There's been no sign of another living
creature for miles.'

'Don't worry, I know this area like the back of
my hand,' he joked, and as if in reflex her gaze
fell to the dark gold hands on the steering wheel.
'A few miles over to our right there's a high
speed dual-carriageway which links the oasis with
the city, but this is the old route.' Tariq smiled
behind his sunglasses. 'It's more interesting.
You'll get some of the flavour of what old-style
desert travel must have been like.'

He was right. Looking at the naked sun-baked
lines of the dunes, it was easy to imagine a camel
train swinging out of the shimmering heat. For

thousands of years the desert had absorbed the high temperatures, and now seemed intent of throwing them back in concentration. Her blazer had been shed long ago, and despite the vehicle's air-conditioner, a film of moisture dampened her brow.

'Me, too,' said Tariq, as she produced a tissue, and she leant across to dab a trickle of sweat from his cheek. 'How's life been at Radio Ras-Al-Khan since I left?'

'Things have steadied off,' she confessed, grinning, 'but Mohammed has matters under control. He's firm, but open-minded. He's already taken over most of Mr Harding's duties.'

'Is Lennie behaving himself?'

'More or less. He never dared go too far with you.' Here she gave another grin. 'But he's still getting Mohammed's measure so he doesn't know whether to try and beat him, or join him.'

The sun's rays burned like laser beams through the windscreen and another trickle of sweat gathered momentum on Tariq's jaw. Without thinking, she reached across to blot it, and he smiled. Their eyes met and clung. Hurriedly Alyssa turned to look out of the window. Platonic friends, he had said. But platonic friends never gazed at each other with such heart-thudding intensity.

'You're wise not to spend too much time by the pool,' he murmured. 'Some European women grill themselves until they resemble well-done steaks, but your skin is the colour of pale honey. Just right.'

Just right for what? she could not help wondering. Just right for him to kiss and caress? She refused to respond to the intimacy which had entered his tone.

'Radio Ras-Al-Khan is much slicker now that——'

Tariq narrowed his eyes against the glare. 'I don't want to talk about Radio Ras-Al-Khan any more, I'd rather talk about you.'

'But you know all about me from my personnel file,' she protested, sitting up a little straighter. 'There's nothing more to tell.'

'There is. For a start you can tell me about your marriage. I find it strange that you've been a widow less than a year and yet rarely mention your husband. Weren't you happy?'

Alyssa stared out through the windscreen at the bare basalt mountains beyond the dunes. 'No, I wasn't,' she admitted.

'Why not?'

She grew tense, disturbed by his forthright manner. 'We were married for the wrong reasons.'

'Which were?'

'My marriage is over, Tariq. I'd rather not——'

'You'd like me to mind my own business?' he asked, his eyes leaving the track to fix on her. He didn't say that maybe she had something to hide, but she felt he inferred it.

'Revelations don't come easy.' She gave a half-hearted smile. 'At least, not the "look at my appendix scar" kind.'

'I didn't mean to pry,' he apologised. 'It's just—well, I'd like to know more about you.'

Alyssa frowned, wondering whether keeping quiet held more danger than offering a censored version of her marriage.

If she made a big issue of refusing information perhaps TGariq would realise something was wrong. She couldn't afford that to happen. Already he'd contacted Jerry Thompson with enquiries about her career, suppose he decided to look further into her personal life?

'Doug and I were married because he needed my flat-footed common sense, my ability to cope come what may. And—and I suppose I had grand ideas of curing him of his ...' she chose the word, '... insecurity.'

'But the relationship didn't work?' She shook her head. 'You've given me the motivation, now give me the facts,' he ordered, as calmly as if some media angle was being discussed.

This invasion of her privacy was horrifying. If she failed to produce a satisfactory account, what then? Suppose Tariq decided she was hedging, suppose he remembered Nigel Dutton's name! A few enquiries at the correct source, and ... Having heard the whole sordid tale, would he allow a woman so deeply, so irretrievably in debt, to continue representing Radio Ras-Al-Khan? Image was important in the media. One whiff of scandal and careers could be ruined. Her career. A swift glance at his face warned Alyssa to be wary of evasions. It was vital she pick her way carefully through the minefield of the past. One false step and...

'Doug and I first met when he was in hospital. I was running a request programme there at the time, and I used to tour the wards to collect record dedications.'

'Why was your husband in hospital?'

'He'd had open heart surgery.'

Tariq digested this. 'So you fell in love?'

'Not then. Doug was just another face. When we met later I didn't recognise him out of his pyjamas.'

'But he recognised you? He must have done.'

'Yes,' she said simply. The mountains were clearer now, grey-brown rock scorching beneath the noon-day sun. 'He'd been discharged from hospital and had started up a private bus company. I was working for the local radio station, and when Doug landed a contract to supply minibuses for outside broadcasts, he looked me up.' She was silent for a moment, involved with her memories. 'Doug moved at a frantic pace, because he'd survived a brush with death,' she said, by way of explanation. 'Within weeks he'd proposed and began pressing me to marry him. I suggested we wait a while, take our time, but he wouldn't accept any delay. It was like being swept up in a whirlwind. With Doug everything had to be now, this minute. His haste flattered me.'

'But you were in love?'

'Yes, yes.' She was relieved Tariq's attention was on the road ahead. Her hands sketched a quick futile gesture. 'I suppose I never really had time to discover exactly how I felt before other issues came crowding in. He reckoned I confused love with—with pity. Maybe he was right.'

Dark brows pulled together. 'Pity?'

'Doug had been starved of affection and somehow that drew me to him. I have this needing to be needed,' Alyssa explained, unconscious bitterness tinging her voice. 'When I was a little girl I was always bringing home cast-off pets and stray animals. A natural do-gooder, that's me! I once found a seagull with a broken wing and badgered my father into making it a cage. Nasty was its name, due to the bird's spiteful temper. I devoted all my spare time to trying to tame the idiotic thing.'

'And did you?'

She made a face. 'Not in the least. I just had pecked fingers. But that's typical. I'm a pushover for the sick, the halt and needy. Big-hearted Alyssa always made a bee-line for the kids no one else wanted to play with. The problem children, the ones with chips on their shoulders.'

'Your husband had a chip on his shoulder?'

'Yes.' She swung to him. 'Can't we just drop this?' she implored, her blue eyes big and troubled. 'The past can't be changed. I'd rather forget.'

'Just tell me once, *habibati*, just once. So I can understand.' A dark-gold hand left the steering wheel to find hers, squeezing her fingers gently. 'Please.'

'So I responded to that part of Doug which needed me.' Alyssa set off again at a rattling pace, determined to get her story over and done with. 'He expected all of my attention as a right. He took all my love, demanded all the caring I had to give, but he was never satisfied. When he'd drained me dry, the accusations started. If another man looked at me, he'd fly into a tantrum.' She paused, recalling the days, the weeks, the months when her husband had been on the brink of falling apart. 'But there were reasons. Doug had so many troubles. His health was a worry, and his business never went well. He'd rushed in there, too.' She stopped dead. Unwittingly she had reached the edge of a precipice, but she would go no further. Tariq must not be allowed the faintest hint of her money troubles. 'And the problem was that I sympathised,' she gabbled, rushing off at a tangent. 'Doug had had a difficult time as a child. His natural parents had mistreated him, then he was shuttled around several lots of foster parents, and finally he was put up for adoption on his sixth birthday.'

'Six?' Tariq winced. 'So he was old enough to know what was happening?'

'Oh yes, he knew all right.' A lump formed in her throat. Whenever she dwelt on the knocks Douglas had suffered, she felt like crying. 'It—it was the classic battered child syndrome. His mother was some flighty girl who hated having a kid to drag around, and his father was a sailor with a vicious streak. He'd come on leave, get roaring drunk, and then beat the hell out of his wife and Doug. Eventually the neighbours alerted the authorities and Doug was sent to a children's home for his own safety. Then came the foster parents, and in due course his own parents lost all interest and decided they'd rather he was adopted.' Alyssa gulped. 'Agnes Brett and her husband found him appealing. From photographs he looked like a downtrodden angel.'

'Why go for a six-year-old, not a baby?'

'Knowing my mother-in-law, I'd guess she hoped to avoid the messy stage,' she said cryptically. 'Sleepless nights and dirty nappies would have horrified her.'

'But six-year-old boys can leave a trail of destruction,' Tariq pointed out. 'Jaber, my nephew, is a prime example.'

Alyssa gave the wisp of a smile. 'I gather most of the fight had been beaten out of Doug at the time the Bretts adopted him. He was very subdued, super-obedient. When he did bounce back, Mr Brett was on hand to direct his energies into the proper channels. He was a stabilising influence, but unfortunately he died when Doug reached ten. By then the little angel had become a common-or-garden schoolboy, and Agnes had tired of the novelty of having a child around. Her affection was thinly spread. Doug wasn't allowed to invite his friends in to play. Agnes went up in smoke if he appeared with dirty knees or torn shirts. Her single aim was to keep life neat and tidy, and she was quite prepared to barter in order to achieve that. A system evolved whereby she'd bribe Doug into behaving by dispensing cash. He never received a hug or a kiss if he was good, he was handed a pound note and sent down to the shops to buy whatever he wanted. Agnes brainwashed him into believing all that mattered was how many material possessions you had, how much money there was in your pocket. Deep down he always knew Agnes didn't give a damn about him.' Alyssa's eyes were bright with unshed tears. 'It was only after we were married that I realised what a distorted view he had of relationships. He could've been buried beneath a mountain of love, but he would never have recognised its existence. Doug never trusted anyone, not even me. So ...' She raised and lowered her hands. 'So I felt sorry for him, and I can't blame him for resenting that. He'd get himself worked up and accuse me of just about every sin under the sun, but afterwards he'd be overcome with remorse and apologise madly. I always forgave him.'

'Did he want forgiveness?'

'I don't know. That's something I've often wondered about myself. Maybe he was trying to goad me into calling a halt. Maybe I should have walked out and administered a short sharp shock. But I didn't. I couldn't risk that because other things had to be considered. Oh,' she dismissed everything with an entirely insincere laugh, 'it doesn't matter now.'

'So your husband was mercenary?'

'Mercenary?' The precipice had been avoided once, but Tariq was pushing her towards the edge again.

'You once said your husband taught you money is important, ultra-important.' His flair for total recall was dismaying. 'Was his business— *hold on tight!*'

His shout propelled Alyssa into lunging for the dashboard safety bar, gripping with both hands. Just in time, for he slammed on the brakes and the Land-Cruiser bounced on to the soft sand like a disrailed roller-coaster. Ahead a brown blur resolved itself into a camel, galloping towards them in a frenzy of rhythm and speed, all knee joints, thudding hooves and curiously jerking neck. The animal was following an erratic path. Left, then right, then left again. Muttering Arabic curses Tariq swerved, but the camel swerved too, making a collision seem inevitable. The animal pounded closer, kicking up sand clouds. Harsher muttered Arabic, then he wrenched at the wheel and the camel lumbered past with inches to spare.

'I never knew they could move so fast,' Alyssa panted, when they had come to a standstill. Heart thumping, she raised a hand to her breast. 'Nor that they were so big and bony in close-up. If only I could have got that pound of hooves on tape!'

They both swivelled, looking through the rear window to watch the camel disappear beyond the crest of a dune. Tariq let out a hiss of relief. He took off his sunglasses and rubbed roughly at his brow.

'Meet one when you're going all out on a main road and you're in the middle of a nasty accident.' His eyes swept worriedly over her. 'Are you okay?'

'I'm fine. Shaken, but not stirred.'

Reassured, he grinned and slid his sunglasses back into place before cautiously switching on the ignition. 'Let's hope we're not up to the axles in sand.' They weren't, not quite, though some skilful manoeuvring was required before he drove them back on to the road. 'I apologise for that

diversion. Obviously some of Ras-Al-Khan's
citizens neglect to read their Highway Code!'

Alyssa grinned. 'Ah, but that was a wild camel.
I'm sure your tame ones have more road sense.'

'I wish I could agree, but unfortunately
there's no such thing as a wild camel. Each has an
owner, no matter if that owner is far, far away.'

They continued their journey, Tariq explaining
some of the laws of the desert, and as he spoke
Alyssa's nerves calmed. Like the camel she, also,
had had a close shave. If the personal questions
had continued, sooner or later she would have
been faced with revealing the truth or resorting to
out and out lies. She had a nasty premonition that
either way would have led to disaster.

In due course the road climbed an escarpment,
levelling off on to a broad gravel plain hemmed in
by the bare mountains. No sand dunes here, just
flat stony land with ribby cattle wandering
amongst stunted tinder-dry trees. At a peeling
white signpost they turned, following a track
which meandered between craggy hillocks. Just
when Alyssa was thinking she had never seen so
much naked rock, such an inhospitable terrain,
they rounded a corner and ahead was a blue
lake—the oasis. In her imagination an oasis had
never been bigger than a duckpond, but the lake
must have been half a mile wide and several miles
long. On the far shore a cluster of dun-coloured
flat-topped houses were surrounded by palm
trees.

'At last, living trees with green leaves!' she
exclaimed.

'That's the village of Ali Obaid and ahead, on

the left bank, is what remains of Suroor's Hanging Gardens. He owns all the land on this side of the water.'

All the land meant a vast sandy acreage and the white lozenge, at which Tariq had flicked his fingers so dismissively, was a speck in the distance. The Land-Cruiser clocked up two more miles before they drew close enough for Alyssa to define lengths of blank white wall, topped with hammered points of black iron. The walls marked out a huge square straddling a promontory, and dead centre sat Suroor's folly. Steel reinforcing rods jutted obscenely from what, at first sight, appeared to be a mutation of igloo and Sleeping Beauty's many-turreted castle.

'Different!' she said, sharing a grin with Tariq as they halted at a deserted gatehouse comprising two smaller igloos which guarded vividly painted steel slab gates.

'There should've been two additional wings,' he told her, speeding along an apology of a drive, the gates solidly padlocked behind them. Ahead, before the half-finished building, was a grassy oval, as unexpected on the sandy waste as a green rug tossed down by a salesman. 'The wings were planned to curve around and virtually enclose the lawn. But Suroor didn't get that far.'

'And a gardener comes each day to keep this patch watered?'

'Yes, though only Suroor and Allah know why. To my mind it's a complete waste of time, money and effort.'

His disgust provoked an amused glance. 'As you've already told Sheikh Suroor?' she grinned.

'Forcibly, but he takes no notice. He and I differ on just about everything. We're not the best of friends, nor ever likely to be.'

Alyssa reached over the seat to find her sunhat. 'Yet he's eager to have you as his son-in-law?' she asked carefully.

Tariq swung the four-wheel-drive beneath a makeshift corrugated iron shelter and braked. 'There are political undertones and *over*tones.' He was sardonic. 'My uncle regards the marriage with Shamsa as a guarantee of my allegiance, although I've already assured him my loyalty to Ras-Al-Khan is beyond doubt. Here, give me your hand.'

The ground was uneven, and when he helped her down from the Land-Cruiser Alyssa could not keep from tottering. Back at the apartment her rush to obey Tariq's command of 'Go and get ready', had resulted in her pulling on the first footwear which had come to hand—white leather sandals with spindly heels, but now she regretted her haste. Around the carcass of the house were piles of gravel, scattered scaffolding poles, nuggets of concrete leftovers. Within a yard or two her sandals were full of sand, and there was the added discomfort of the burn of the sunbaked earth through the thin soles. Trying not to fidget too noticeably from one foot to the other, Alyssa listened as Tariq revealed what the original blueprint had contained.

'Latticed walls would have enclosed a swimming pool, patio and gardens,' he said, taking her around to the rear of the building. 'Suroor professes to be a gardening freak, so

there were long discussions with nurserymen
before he arranged for planeloads of plants to be
flown in. But when the economics hit home he
lost interest. Everything was left to die.' Tariq
pointed a scornful finger at the withered remains
of what appeared to have been a mass of
oleanders. 'As usual he did things the wrong way
round. The gardens were landscaped before the
house was built, and when everything fell
through he didn't even bother to give instructions
for the plants to be dug up and replanted at his
palace in Ras-Al-Khan.'

Gamely Alyssa marched beside him. The sun
was dazzling, reflected up from the sand, and she
was sweaty again. Her blouse was sticking to her
back. When they rounded a corner, she smiled.
Between the charred remains of a bonfire and
some battered diesel cans, a hibiscus bloomed, its
scarlet blossoms as vivid as young girls in organza
party dresses.

'Look, a survivor!'

Grinning, Tariq strode forward to pluck off
one of the flowers, but when he came back to her
his grin had faded. Gravely he removed her
sunhat. The simple gesture seemed to stop the
world from revolving, and Alyssa forgot the
glare, the sticky heat, how much her feet hurt. All
she could see was the look in his eyes. With
infinite tenderness he tucked the blossom into her
hair.

'Placing a flower behind one ear means you're
available, but behind the other means you're not.
Have I got it right?'

Straight away she removed the blossom and

twirled it between her fingers, touching the delicate petals.

'But I'm not available, am I?' she asked quietly, raising her head to challenge him.

Tariq licked his lips. 'No,' he agreed, after a moment. 'No, you're not. Not for me.'

She wanted him to take her in his arms. Wanted him to be at the other end of the earth. She wanted this moment to last for ever. Wanted it to end right now. She hated him. She loved him. Blindly she set off, stumbling on the thin heels, shaking free of his hand when he reached out to steady her. She flung the scarlet blossom away, not caring where it fell.

'My feet are on fire,' she said, marching round to the front of the house. 'And I'm all sweaty and—and I wish your uncle had got as far as the swimming pool because right now I can think of nothing I'd like better than to be immersed in cold water. Preferably with an iceberg or two for company,' she added, hoping to channel her distress into humour.

'I can't provide an iceberg, but I know how to cool you down,' Tariq said, when they reached the porch. 'Hold on a minute, then we'll go inside.'

He strode back to the Land-Cruiser where he collected a couple of large coolboxes. Alyssa used his absence to good effect, and by the time he returned to unlock the door, she was calm again. He stood aside for her to enter, and cool air met them.

'Don't tell me the house is permanently air-conditioned?' she exclaimed.

'And fully furnished, with all mod cons,' he said drily. 'Suroor never does things by half.'

Alyssa paused to remove her sandals, then padded with childlike pleasure around the cool marble floor of the entrance hall.

'Bliss!'

Tariq laughed, then removed his own shoes, joining her in the middle of the square room which also did duty as a portrait gallery. Large paintings of members of the Al Zahini family hung on the walls. She picked out Sheikh Ahmad, Karim, and Sheikh Suroor was present in three different poses, but Alyssa could find no picture of Tariq. Presumably that would come once he had proved his worthiness by marrying Shamsa?

'Why has half a house been made fit to live in?' she enquired, knowing that if she was to survive she had better talk rather than dwell on Tariq's future, his *married* future.

He hoisted a coolbox into each fist. 'Because on special occasions, such as Eid holidays, Suroor receives the men from Ali Obaid village here. Or that's his excuse.' The derision was thick. 'It'd be far cheaper to send out a fleet of cars and transport them to his palace in the city, rather than keeping this place on the go, air-conditioning and all, but he can't see it that way. Or won't.'

'Though you've argued the point?' she teased.

'I have mentioned it in passing,' Tariq agreed with a smile.

He led the way into a large room where the walls were covered in green watered silk. The furnishings were an odd mix. There was a dining table and chairs in the Chippendale style, a massive stainless steel and smoked glass wall unit, powder-blue silk settees covered in heavy-duty plastic. Alyssa swivelled, her eyes lurching drunkenly from an onyx table held aloft by two bronze stags to a criss-cross display of flintlock rifles.

'Something for everyone,' Tariq commented, noticing her surprise, then he opened the door on a far smaller room. The bizarre clash of tastes had ceased, for this was an airy place of pastel shades, and plants and sunshine. The carpet which covered the floor was in clear lemon, white and pale beige, the colour of a Siamese cat, while the walls were lemon, too. Fresh semi-sheer nets covered wide windows overlooking the rear of the house. There were no plastic-covered settees or ornate tables; just masses of cushions embroidered in lemon, white and lime. 'This is my hideaway,' he explained. 'I turfed out the *objets d'art*, so when the gardener's brother comes in he cleans the room in two seconds flat. I'm hooked on simplicity, though it could be an over-reaction to the rest of the house.'

'You just stretch out on the cushions?'

He nodded as he set down the cool boxes. 'Dining *al fresco*'s impossible in the Gulf in summer, so I do the next best thing and picnic in here. This one——' he patted a box, 'holds today's lunch, but here is something especially for you.' With a flourish he unfastened the lid and from a bed of ice produced a dark green bottle.

'Champagne!' Alyssa laughed.

'I remembered how much you enjoy it,' he said, giving a broad wink.

'But are you going to drink champagne, too?'

Tariq was unpacking the glasses. 'Yes. Why not?'

'Well, I thought—er, with you becoming a Muslim and Muslims being reticent about drinking alcohol. Well . . .' Alyssa felt awkward. She wished she had never raised the subject.

'But I'm not a Muslim, so I'm breaking no laws. Now, can I pop the cork without getting you, me and the carpet soaked?' Lower lip pushed out in concentration, he bent to grip the bottle between his knees, and after peeling off the foil pushed at the cork with his thumbs. There was a resounding 'pop' and he rapidly filled the two glasses which she had pushed at him. Together they sat amongst the pillows. 'A toast to my favourite pin-up,' he said, raising his glass.

Alyssa's heart stopped beating. That look was back in his dark eyes, the look which made her skin prickle so familiarly, so alarmingly. Refusing to respond, she rested an elbow back on a pillow, stretched out her legs, wiggled her toes, and gave a little cough. If she concentrated on the champagne, and looked everywhere but at the golden-skinned male beside her, perhaps she had a chance at survival.

'Do something for me.' Tariq was studying her. 'Tilt back your head and turn. Now smile.'

She would have preferred to refuse, but refusing seemed churlish. She shifted on to one hip and produced a doubtful smile. 'Like this?'

'Mmm.' He set down his glass and leant

forward to loosen the chiffon scarf. 'Let's take this off and then——'

'Tariq,' she murmured in low protest.

'Let me.' His voice was husky, throbbing with emotion. Reaching out, he pulled the chiffon free and began to arrange her hair around her shoulders, sliding his fingers through its silky tangle. 'That's how I've thought of you all week. I have a confession. I kept the newspaper photograph.'

'You pinned it over your bed?' she joked, failing to mask her dismay. 'I had the impression you didn't approve of the teasing minx.'

'No, no,' he replied distractedly.

She needed to throw a dash of cold water. 'I'm not a minx, Tariq. Neither do I tease.'

'I know.' His eyes met hers. 'I know you're not out for——' With a growl of self-disgust, he swept to his feet. He grabbed his glass and strode to where the billowy white net obscured the windows. His stance was erect and aggressive. The look he shot back over his shoulder was aggressive, too. 'You wanted to cool down, so go.' A hand was jabbed towards a door on his left. 'There's a shower through there. Use it. Cool down. While you do, I'll set out our lunch.'

He had given a harsh command. Tariq wanted her out of his sight. He wanted her away from him, and she knew why.

'As you say, sir.' Alyssa wondered how she could sound jaunty at a time like this.

He gulped down the remainder of his champagne. '*Imshi!*' he growled, desperate for her to be gone. He looked down at the empty goblet suspended between his fingers, then raised his head. 'Go, please *go*. Can't you see that I want you so much that——' In a gesture of sheer frustration, he raised a muscled arm and hurled the glass into a distant corner, where it shattered into a thousand diamond slivers. 'That if you don't go away I'll *rape* you! All week I've tormented myself with thoughts of you. I don't want Shamsa,' he muttered. 'She's a giggling schoolgirl and I don't want a schoolgirl. I want a woman, with a woman's body, a woman's needs.' He raked a rough hand through his hair. 'I want *you*. And you want me, Alyssa. We both want each other, yet we're stuck in the middle of this damned awful situation where——' He turned his back to glower out of the window. 'Just go away and have a shower, or do whatever the hell you want. Just go. Just give me a chance to—Just go,' Tariq pleaded.

CHAPTER NINE

ALYSSA sped into the bathroom. Hands covering her face, several deep breaths were needed before she could throw herself into undressing with a speed akin to frenzy. She must keep active, must do *something* while so many emotions were unravelling themselves in her head. She and Tariq had been playing at brinkmanship, that much was crystal clear. The zing between them was almost tangible, a declaration of overwhelming physical attraction. Knowing that, why had he invited her out? More to the point, why had she accepted? Because, because . . . Because desire has damn-all to do with common sense. That zing had been a signal. They had been sending signals back and forth with increasing urgency ever since their first sight of each other.

'Fools, the pair of us,' she muttered, and resolutely ejected further thoughts on the subject from her head.

Compact and prettily tiled in lemon, with occasional hand-painted sprawls of wild poppies, Suroor's dubious taste had not held sway in the bathroom. Here all modern indulgences from three-cornered Roman tub to bidet were included, and an open mirrored bi-fold door revealed shelved storage space where fluffy lemon towels waited to be used. Chunky flagons sat on a vanity unit, and Alyssa counted among them bath salts, shower gel, body lotions and talcs. Even shower caps were provided, so she peeled one from its sachet and yanked it over her head, bundling her hair out of sight.

The water was not ice-cold, nor had she expected ice-cold water in the middle of the desert, but it was cool enough to be refreshing. Arms stretched upwards, eyes shut tight, she stood beneath the fine jet, chastised by the sting of the water. The heat and perspiration were slooshed off, and the fevered scorch of her senses began to cool. Sanity returned but only briefly, for the shower door opened behind her. Dark-gold arms slid around her waist and she was pulled back against a naked male body. Her composure gurgled down the drain.

'Forgive me. I'm only a man,' Tariq said brokenly into her neck. 'I can't ... I can't stop myself. I can't keep away from you. I know we shouldn't start something we can't finish, but——'

She stood as still as a statue, though her heart rolled dementedly. 'Tariq, no! You're soon to be married, and I—I don't want to get involved, so making love is ... forbidden.'

'I know. I know all the reasons why this is wrong, and I thought I had the self-control to keep things platonic between us, but I don't. If we'd met in the West, it would be different. I wouldn't be under this pressure, there wouldn't be all these restrictions.'

'But we're not in the West.'

'If we were, would you sleep with me?'

'That's hypothetical,' Alyssa wailed, for he was playing a dangerous game.

His arms tightened around her. 'Would you?'

Oh God! she thought, I love him. And if there was some glorious world where he wasn't going to marry Shamsa and Nigel Dutton didn't exist . . .

'*Yes!* Yes, yes, I would.' She thrust the words at him by the forkful. 'Now are you satisfied?'

'No, I'm not, and neither are you.' His hand moved upwards to cup her breasts where glossy rivulets streaked across the honey-coloured skin. 'Why shouldn't we do what we're craving to do? No one knows we're here at the oasis and we'll be gone long before the gardener arrives. Why should we feel guilty when we both know what we feel about each other?'

'Do we?' Alyssa floated the question like a frail paper boat on the ocean.

'You must know I'm crazy about you. Didn't someone once say, "To speak of love is to make love"? I spoke of love the third time I saw you. I was angry and suspicious, but that was because I resented the hold you already seemed to have over my senses. I've wanted you ever since.'

'Balzac.'

'I beg your pardon?'

'Balzac said it.'

Tariq laughed, but then grew defiant. 'So what's wrong about us making love? No, don't answer that. But just for today?' His palm polishing her wet breast was making it difficult for Alyssa to keep still. 'Just for today, *habibati*?' he asked softly.

Physical need and common sense unhappily collikded. Was she resilient enough to love him for just one day? Love and live on, pretending this time at the oasis was an aberration, a ships-that-pass-in-the-night kind of thing? She had never indulged in casual sex, always scorned those who did, but the bond of passion which existed between her and Tariq was different. *Different!* She nearly moaned out loud at the trite excuse. Wasn't that the standard self-defence of every woman who allowed herself to be seduced? There was no danger that she would become pregnant, Alyssa thought, hating her practicality. Nightmarishly afraid of Nigel Dutton forcing her to submit, she had continued with birth control precautions since Douglas's death.

Wasn't it preferable to make love with Tariq once than never? Yes, her body screamed. Yes, yes, *yes*. 'I'm only a man,' he had said, echoing her own words, yet he was a man capable of fighting tigers. She could not fight tigers, she could not fight him.

He appeared to sense that her inward struggle had ended, for he nuzzled into her neck, helping himself to tender bites, telling her of his need, how they would journey to paradise and back.

'You're so beautiful,' he murmured, and the insistent movement of his hands—gliding across the hard nubs of her breasts, searching out the flatness of her stomach, the ripeness of her thighs—was irresistible.

With a helpless moan of pleasure she leant back, her head against his shoulder. Then a thought struck, and Alyssa jerked upright.

'I can't! I refuse to make love while I'm wearing a shower cap.'

With a bellow of joyous laughter, Tariq scooped her up into his arms and kissed her, his mouth warm and eager as the water thrummed down. Diamond drips sparkled on his shoulders, in his hair, amongst the bristles of his moustache.

'Alyssa Brett, I love you,' he crowed. 'And I promise that the minute you've finished washing me we'll remove that shower cap.' He set her back on her feet, reaching for a tablet of soap. 'I'm hot and sticky, and you're my slave girl. Aren't you? Just for today?'

'Just for today,' she agreed, having little difficulty in justifying her decision beneath his cajoling smile.

She began to lather him, rubbing the soap across his chest. Sleeked down with the water, his body hair was like black lace over dark-gold satin. Being naked with Tariq felt natural, exciting though it was. No restraint existed on either side. With him she could be herself, there was no need to hold back as there had been with Douglas. Tariq was a healthy, muscular man, an animal in his prime. He would make love as vibrantly as he did everything else in life, and with the same finesse. But she must remember that he was hers just for today.

'You can do below the waist yourself,' Alyssa said, patting him lightly on the backside. 'I'm getting cold.'

'Did your nerve fail?' he teased, as she stepped from beneath the plume of water and wrapped a towel around herself. Tariq soaped, washed and sluiced himself in seconds. A few rough strokes dried him, and then he knotted a towel at his hips, sarong-style. 'Perhaps it's as well. My self-control's a wee bit precarious.' He grinned. 'You washed me, so now I'll dry you. That's an order, slave girl.'

'Yes, master.'

'Face me.' The command was husky, and when he looked down on her full breasts his equilibrium faltered. Without warning they were clasped together in a damp, heated tangle of flesh and towels, mouth pressed into mouth, supple body against supple body.

'Let's try and slow things down,' he gulped, coming up for air. 'I hate to have to remind you again, but I'm only a man.'

'And I'm still wearing my shower cap!' Alyssa exclaimed, wondering how on earth she could have forgotten *that*.

'Allow me.'

Tariq pulled the plastic bonnet free, smiling as the heavy ashen hair tumbled on to her shoulders. He found a comb and began to tidy the tousled mop. Dedicated to the task, the tip of his tongue protruding between his teeth, he revealed yet another side of himself. What a complex man he is, Alyssa realised. East and West. An aggressive game hunter who knows the world's a jungle, yet a man capable of great sensitivity. Did Shamsa realise how fortunate she was? Alyssa closed her mind. All that mattered was *here*, *now*.

She reached up to kiss a bead of water from his moustache, and the hair combing was forgotten as their torsos twisted together again. His mouth met hers, mutual urgency making her rock into him, hands clawing at his waist for support. Her breasts were eager for his touch and when he pulled apart, bending his dark head to her body, she sighed.

Somehow they moved into the carpeted room to lie among the pillows. Tariq held her close. Dry now, her skin throbbed with heat and expectancy. She ran her hands across the breadth of his shoulders. He was so well-muscled, so powerful, so well-endowed.

He moved down her body to kiss the hollow of her navel, then slowly and deliberately ran his tongue up between her breasts, making a delicious detour to encircle each quivering nipple before he resumed his journey to the silken column of her throat, and finally her mouth. Another deep, deep kiss before he bent again. What he was doing, the scour of his moustache across her skin, the gentle bite of his teeth, made her weak with desire and she clung, nails marking his flesh, head snapped back.

'Darling,' Alyssa murmured. 'My darling.'

Now she moved, pushing Tariq back on to the pillows so that her mouth could rouse *him*, her lips and her tongue make *him* gasp and shudder in ecstasy.

'Oh God!' he groaned, unable to wait any longer.

He thrust into her, moving with such fiercely controlled deliberation that a series of inward explosions racked her body, making her cry out. Muscles corded, Tariq ground closer, deeper, penetrating with increasing urgency. All control snapped. Together they clung, transmitting desire from one to another until a massive mutual explosion blasted them out of this world into the heavens where all was peace and calm and deep, deep satisfaction.

Careless of the day passing, they lay together and when they made love a second time, it was different—a stronger, more assured enjoyment of each other's body. Tariq was gentle, yet marvellously passionate. Instinctively he knew how best to please her. But she also knew how to please him, Alyssa thought dreamily, her eyelids closing. He held her until she was asleep, then left her side, returning to cover her with a light blanket. For over an hour Tariq stood by the window, deep in thought.

The room was steeped in the mellow golden light of the setting sun when she awoke. Rubbing her eyes, Alyssa pushed herself up on to her elbow. By the window Tariq made a dark silhouette. He was back in his jeans, though his chest was bare.

'How long have I been asleep?' she asked.

'Long enough, *habibati*. We must be on our way.'

She sat up, leaving the blanket behind. 'I don't want to go. I don't want this day to finish.'

'Neither do I,' he murmured, walking towards her. His smile was melancholy as he squatted down on his haunches to touch her cheek with his fingertips. 'I can't even say when we'll be able to come here again. There are arrangements to be made now. Everything is different. I have no

wish to offend anyone, so we must step carefully.
From now on our relationship must——'

'Stop,' she implored, shaking her head. 'Don't
talk.' She leant forward to press her cheek
against his, feeling the warmth, the faint scratch
of his beard shadow, smelling the fresh scrubbed
smell of him. 'Kiss me one last time before we
go.'

He kissed her, plunging a hand into the
lustrous curtain of her hair. The embrace was
rough and passionate, but when he made as if to
stand Alyssa twisted her arms around his neck,
her naked breasts hot against him.

'Get dressed, *habibati*.' More a plea than a
request, Tariq almost choked on the words.

'Soon.'

Arching her body towards him, she moved so
that the tips of her breasts caught against the dark
mat of hair. Alyssa rubbed her mouth against the
dark-gold of his shoulders, kissing with parted
lips as she tasted his skin. With a groan, Tariq
allowed himself to be captured and when his
mouth opened on hers, his kiss was that of a
starving man. His hands moved in a frenzied
renewal of their knowledge of her body, stroking
the soft curves, the plateaux, the crevices. He
moaned a protest at what he was doing, but
nothing could stop this gathering passion and
Alyssa sighed as he propelled her downwards on
to the pillows.

Summer sunsets in the Gulf are shortlived, and
the sky was deep orange, shot with translucent
mother-of-pearl, by the time they climbed back

into the four-wheel drive. Tariq had driven out through the steel gates and was reclamping the padlock, when she noticed him come to attention. Following his frown, she twisted to see a robed figure coming towards them on a bicycle. This had to be the gardener! Alyssa did not know what to do. Diving down flat on the seat was a little belated because the man was only yards away, and with her hair flowing down her back in skeins of silver-gold she had no hope at all of appearing anonymously local. She sat as if of stone, but he still saw her, nearly falling off his bike when he realised Tariq had a companion. He dismounted and continued to gawp while a few words in Arabic were exchanged.

'Let's go,' Tariq said, jumping in beside her. Brutally he slammed into first gear and they shot away, leaving a dust-cloud to settle around the wide-eyed gardener. 'Maybe I should have paid him off,' he muttered to himself. 'No, why the hell should I?'

Back through the desert they drove, each absorbed in their own thoughts. Languid from their lovemaking, Alyssa had no wish for words. Words meant analysing what had taken place, and tomorrow was soon enough for that. The sky was black and stars shone overhead when they reached Ras-Al-Khan. Tariq avoided the Colonnade's brightly lit entrance, instead pulling on to the shadowy car park. He cut the engine and turned.

'We're not supposed to kiss in public, but——' He reached across to claim her lips, then sat back soberly. 'I've been planning what we must do.

Regrettably I leave at the crack of dawn tomorrow for a few days in Oslo, but the minute I return we'll organise ourselves and——'

'Let's talk when you come back,' Alyssa begged, forbidding him to break the spell. 'When you come back.'

Tonight she needed the cushion of his love. She did not want to face reality. After another kiss she left him and went up to her apartment. The 'phone started to ring as she unlocked the door, and Alyssa sighed. If this was Brough he could take a running jump, likewise Lennie.

'Yes?' she asked wearily.

'Lyss?' The line crackled. 'It's me, Meg.'

The dreamlike daze evaporated at a stroke. This was no social call. Something urgent must have happened for Meg to ring long distance. Married to a young and poorly-paid draughtsman, with two small children to feed and clothe, her sister watched the pennies.

'What's—what's the matter?' Surprise and a sickening premonition of disaster had Alyssa stammering.

'Nigel Dutton's been round to the house, and——'

'Look, this is obviously going to be a long call, so I'll ring you back,' she interrupted. 'You mustn't pay.'

'I don't care about the stupid cost of the stupid 'phone call, Lyss,' her sister cried. 'Nigel Dutton knows you're abroad. He made me tell him. And he's threatening to go to the police. I know you owe him money, but—but he says it's twenty thousand pounds! It's not, is it?'

'More or less.'

'What!' Meg's distress would have shattered glass.

'Replace the receiver, and I'll call you straight back. In the meantime calm down, there's a love, and then you can tell me exactly what's happened.' Alyssa's voice was firm. The crunch had come as, inevitably, it had to come, yet in a strange way she felt relieved. There was the sensation of being outside herself, looking on. She was cool and calm, the young woman who always coped. With steady fingers she dialled the number. 'Okay, start at the beginning.'

'There was a bomb scare at the London radio station where you told Nigel Dutton you'd be working,' Meg began. 'The building had to be evacuated, and you weren't there.'

She frowned. 'So?'

'Well, it was reported on television. Cliff and I saw your pal, Jerry Thompson, being interviewed together with other members of the staff. The scare turned out to be a hoax, as they often do, but apparently Nigel Dutton caught the same news bulletin. He noted your absence. He must have thought something was fishy because he contacted the station. They said you didn't work there, never had. He stormed round to see me about an hour ago. Cliff's at work, so I was alone with the kids, and——' An offshoot of Alyssa's brain did a sum and worked out how the time difference made it late afternoon in England. 'And I can't help it, but I always get the jitters when that horrible man speaks to me. I tried to cover for you, Lyss. Honest I did.' Her sister was almost sobbing. 'I pretended you'd been ill, that the job had been postponed but that you'd be reporting for duty any day now, but he accused me of lying. He said I'd been lying to him for months, and that there was no point hoping to fool him any longer. He said I was an accessory.'

'Meg, you're not! This business is between me and him, it has nothing to do with you. He was trying to scare you, that's all.'

'And he succeeded,' her sister said mournfully.

Alyssa's stomach twisted. She was responsible for Meg suffering like this. 'I'm so very, very sorry you've had to come up against Nigel Dutton. I never imagined he'd attack *you*.' She reached a rapid decision. Meg must not be left to bear the brunt of Dutton's anger. 'First thing tomorrow I'll book a flight home. I'll come and sort things out.'

'Supposing you can't?' her sister suggested in a small voice. 'He was absolutely furious. He's a vindictive type, Lyss, and——'

'Don't worry. Once he realises I'm earning such good money, Nigel Dutton'll be willing to allow me more time to pay off the debt.'

What a splendid display of Dutch courage, Alyssa thought after her sister had rung off. Meg had accepted the assurance, as she always accepted her assurances. Meg might be three years older, yet she was the one who panicked while Alyssa stayed calm and coped. But there was a limit to her coping. Jamming a fist against her brow, she rubbed hard, blinking back tears. She was tired of being strong, weary of carrying her burdens alone. She needed someone to depend on. She wanted Tariq's arms around her, holding her close, telling her he would make everything right. But she might as well wish for the moon. Tariq was not hers, never would be hers. Tariq belonged to Shamsa.

Twenty thousand miserable pounds! Without it her life was due to be wrecked, yet what did the sum represent to Tariq? Pocket money? Small change? He never flaunted his wealth, yet it was there in the Baume et Mercier watch he wore on his wrist, there in the solid gold cigarette case, there in his choice of car. Suppose she battened down her pride and asked for his help? Alyssa laughed bitterly. Approaching Tariq was a cruel joke. After their lovemaking today, *especially* after their lovemaking, she could never ask him for money. Not even a loan. If she did, she would be setting herself up fairly and squarely, as the blonde temptress who sold herself for cash. How he would despise her! She would rather die than see disillusionment in those fine dark eyes.

Alyssa hardly slept at all that night. For hours she tossed and turned, screwing the sheet around her as she mind-scripted her meeting with Nigel Dutton. Long before dawn she accepted the cold hard truth—that the only way of repulsing him was to appear with a cheque in her hand to pay off the debt in full. So, she had a choice. She could either submit to the man whose beady little eyes crawled over her in blatant lust, or she could allow Douglas's memory to be assaulted and vilified in open court.

The next morning she went to see Mohammed,

explaining how a crisis demanded her presence in England.

'My mother's ill,' she said, the lie tasting like bitter aloes on her tongue. 'It's touch and go.'

Mohammed saw her strained expression, the dark rings below her eyes, and promptly gave permission for a week's compassionate leave.

'Don't worry, Brough and Lennie can carry the can. Two more of your programmes are already lined up?' She gave her confirmation. 'If we should be pushed, we'll ask that American woman to come and assist. When do you intend to fly out?'

'Today's too short notice to get a flight, so it'll be first thing tomorrow morning.'

'Don't worry,' he repeated. 'Things often aren't as bad as they seem.'

If only he knew! The likelihood of her returning was remote, but Alyssa decided to say nothing and keep her options open for now. But what did she do about Tariq? He would have already left for Oslo, but wasn't that for the best? I love him, she wailed silently. You might love him, a little voice sneered inside her head, but he's not going to spoil his future by returning the emotion in any acceptable form. When he had spoken about them organising themselves, he had only been intent on putting their illicit lovemaking on a regular basis. No thank you! Maybe her unscheduled departure was heaven-sent as far as their relationship was concerned. This way she left with dignity. If by some fluke she did return, she would be forced to tell him that even if he was crazy about her, and her about him, she was not so crazy as to consider becoming his mistress.

The day was a scramble. News of her mother's imaginary illness circulated like wildfire so, in addition to booking an air ticket and finalising as much radio material as she could, she had to deal with a constant stream of wellwishers. Having to lie when everyone was so concerned made her feel lousy, but there was no alternative. After lunch Mr Harding, who was now in his final days, rang to say he had been asked to go and take his leave of Sheikh Suroor, and that she was to accompany him.

'Why me?' Alyssa questioned.

'Heaven knows. Perhaps he saw you on television the other night and fancies a look at you. Suroor's a funny old bloke. The media's never been under his jurisdiction and yet from time to time I've been called in to listen to some obscure suggestion. Gets bees in his bonnet, does Suroor. Mad keen on something for five minutes then—whoof!—loses interest. But with him being heir to the sheikhdom, it pays to kowtow. Otherwise he might say, "Off with your head".'

Within seconds of being admitted into Sheikh Suroor's presence, Alyssa realised he would have liked nothing better than to have been able to say, 'Off with *her* head.' Ushered into his office alone, she sat down at the movement of a doughy hand thick with rings, and waited. Suroor was a fat man, with a bloated face and sallow skin. He studied her for a long time, passionless eyes hooded like a falcon's, then rearranged his bulk in the velvet padded chair and sniffed. When he deigned to speak, it was with a heavy accent which required every ounce of Alyssa's concentration to enable her to understand.

'I regret you must leave Ras-Al-Khan so soon after your arrival,' he said. 'But that is your own doing.'

'I beg your pardon?' She tried to work out what he meant, then realised he must have been informed that she was taking so-called compassionate leave. My word, she thought, news does travel fast.

'And you will not return.'

'I beg your pardon?' Alyssa said a second time.

'You will not return. We do not wish you to return.' She was confused. His English was poor. Had he got something the wrong way round? 'We do not want you in Ras-Al-Khan,' he continued, when she frowned.

'I—I don't understand.'

'Your contract has been terminated. We do not want you here,' Suroor insisted again.

'But I understood my work was of value to radio here,' she protested, too troubled to remember to kowtow. The prospect of her returning might be remote but a blank dismissal was quite a different matter. Okay, it was a bleak chance that Nigel Dutton would agree to her continuing to pay him off a month at a time, but suppose he did? How could she possibly clear the debt unless she was working for Radio Ras-Al-Khan? 'Sheikh Tariq said how pleased he was with my programmes and——'

'Tariq does not want you here.'

Alyssa stared at the fat potentate in dismay.
'But——'

If this dismissal was Tariq's doing, surely he
would have broken the news to her himself?
Then her stomach plunged, for in a flash she
understood. He had risked making love at the
oasis only because he had fixed her dismissal for
today, during his absence. That explained his
insistence that their love be 'just for today'. She
chewed at her lip. No, that couldn't be right.
Tariq would never stoop to anything so under-
hand. He wasn't an opportunist, he *couldn't* be.
'But ... I ... It doesn't make sense,' she
muttered.

'Preparations for his marriage ceremony
commence the day my nephew returns from
Oslo. No longer will he involve himself with
radio matters or radio people.' The sheikh leant
forward. 'You understand?'

The erratic thump of her heart told Alyssa she
did. Suroor was warning her off. He knew about
their visit to the oasis.

'Yes, I do,' she said tightly.

'However, you will not go away empty-
handed,' he continued. 'I understand the major
part of your contract has yet to run, so you will
receive an *ex gratia* payment. Is twenty thousand
pounds satisfactory?' Alyssa blinked. The words
seemed to come from far off, but suddenly they
burst into her brain like shooting stars. 'Is that
satisfactory?' snapped Suroor.

Near hysterical laughter threatened to escape.
Was twenty thousand pounds satisfactory? Was
it? Was it? She did believe in miracles. Now she

was safe from Nigel Dutton's clutches. Now Doug could rest in peace. The sheikh might look like a fat Satan, but he was an angel in disguise.

'Yes, yes,' she said, for he was waiting for an answer.

His hand moved in dismissal. 'My secretary has the money ready.'

'Thank you, thank you.' Alyssa's smile flashed with manic energy. She felt like plunging across the desk and smothering him in grateful kisses.

Suroor gave a sour grimace. 'I see both of us are suited, Mrs Brett. How gratifying.'

CHAPTER TEN

WEARING tights again felt strange. Alyssa stood by the window, consciously stiff-legged and strait-jacketed. Outside the day was crisp. An autumn breeze was housewife-busy, hoovering leaves from the trees, sucking them up and around in a twirl of flame, copper and gold. Catching sight of Cliff, across the yard in the car park, she smiled. Involved in a mutual game of discretion they might be, but her brother-in-law was her friend. He had accepted the explanation of her debt and the swift appearance of twenty thousand pounds, knowing it could not be as glib as she had made it appear. Yet he had not pried, not asked searching questions. As always he had respected her unspoken wish that the past, and especially Douglas's role in the past, remain unexamined.

She returned his thumbs-up of encouragement and watched when he became a male Jane Fonda, exercising his arms up and down, making them 'burn' in an attempt to keep warm. The temperature was low. Alyssa needed the indigo sweater, tweed skirt and cape, but she would have preferred not to be swaddled. Knee-high tan leather boots had taken the place of strappy sandals, a drastic change, and despite having only been back in England for two days, nostalgia for the heat of the Arabian Gulf swelled.

'Mr Dutton will see you now.' The receptionist broke into her thoughts. 'First door on the left.'

Nigel Dutton was as lethal as she remembered him. After greeting her in a manner which contrived to be both chummy and insidious, he wriggled deep into his swivel-chair, mentally ripped off all her clothes, and treated her to the crocodile smile. 'Now I have you where I want you,' the gloating look seemed to say and though, for propriety's sake, he managed to thank her for the cheques she had sent and force out a couple of trite remarks about the weather, he was unable to resist brandishing his cudgel.

'What a wicked little girl you've been, pretending you were in London when all the while you were out in the Middle East. That wasn't very nice.' The crocodile smile showed teeth. 'Or smart.'

'I knew I could earn far more abroad,' Alyssa replied. 'And my single motive in going was to be able to pay back the money as quickly as possible. I'm anxious to clear my debt.'

Her *sang froid* took the edge off his complacency. The beady eyes narrowed and she guessed he had expected her to reappear whitefaced and chastened, ready to throw herself on his mercy.

'Don't fret too much about the cash,' he smirked, deciding her calm was surface show. 'I could still be persuaded to softpedal on payments. I'm not an ogre. And if you play your cards right . . .'

He floated the idea up into the air like a soap bubble, but Alyssa produced a pin.

'You still want me to sleep with you?' she questioned, in her clear, schools' broadcasting voice.

Astonishment jerked Nigel Dutton from his crocodile slumber. They were closeted in his office, but the walls were thin, not much more than partitions. He struggled from the depths of his chair to wag a cautious finger.

'Shh! Someone in the corridor could have heard you.'

'But that's what you have in mind?' she insisted. 'You want me based in London so that you can come down for a dirty weekend whenever it's convenient?'

'You're very outspoken,' he remonstrated, ears pricked for any footsteps outside. He cleared his throat, adjusted his golf club tie, and attempted to manoeuvre himself back into the dominant position. 'How about us taking a little drive in the country? I'll buy you lunch and we can talk in private.'

'Sorry, but my brother-in-law's waiting. I don't have much time to spare.'

The purplish tinge of his face heightened. 'Now, look here!'

'I'd like to get matters clear.' Alyssa flashed an air hostess smile. 'I think we can take it as read that you don't want me to return to the Gulf and work hard to pay off the debt by regular instalments?'

'No.' He recovered a little. 'I'm sure you'd be happier in London, working for that radio station.'

'Don't you mean installed as your mistress?'

Nigel Dutton flinched. 'My word, you believe in calling a spade a spade.'

'Not at all. I can think of a far blunter description of what you intend to happen. I'd say you're coercing me into——'

'We know where we stand,' he scowled. 'Don't forget you still owe me thousands of pounds, and so far I've been very patient.'

'But that patience has its limits, and if I don't do as you ask then there's an ultimatum?'

'Not exactly an ultimatum,' he blustered, then stopped short as his mean streak reasserted itself. 'Either you pay up, or you establish yourself in London and—and we can meet up for dinner from time to time.'

'Be your mistress?' she encouraged.

He didn't like her to be so explicit, but—'*Yes*, be my mistress.'

'And if I don't pay up and I don't agree to be London-based?'

'Then I shall have no alternative but to initiate legal proceedings. I can guarantee that husband of yours won't come out of a court case smelling of roses,' he could not resist sneering. 'It's your choice.'

Alyssa unzipped her shoulder-bag and produced a brown-paper bundle. 'In that case, I'll pay up. Would you ask your cashier to come in, please? I'd like him to count the money in my presence, and I'll need a receipt.'

'Where did you get that?' Nigel Dutton demanded, shooting forward, his eyes about to spring from their sockets. The purplish tinge deepened to vermilion as Alyssa took out another bundle of notes, and another.

She pretended she had not heard. 'Would you call in the cashier?'

The pay-off transaction was delicious, though she knew she hammed it up shamefully. Stacking the bundles in a straight line, she counted them off one by one, like a sergeant major taking roll call. When the cashier had departed, and the receipt was safely in her possession, she rose to her feet.

'I'd be grateful for your assurance that the matter is now closed, permanently?'

'Maybe, but there again, maybe not. Suppose I decide to spread tales about what a failure your husband really was?' he taunted.

'There were reasons for Douglas's failures,' she replied, determined to deny him a riot of denunciation.

'Reasons!' Nigel Dutton spat out an expletive. 'For a smart young woman you have an incredible blind spot where Douglas is concerned. Suppose I do talk? What then?'

Alyssa walked over to the door. 'You won't talk,' she said, and opened her gloved hand to reveal a tiny tape recorder. 'Because if you talk, so shall I. And you wouldn't want Mrs Dutton to hear all your plans about setting up a love nest in London, now would you?'

Common sense told her she should be happy. Common sense told her she should forget the traumas of the past and put everything behind her. She was young, healthy, talented, and she did not owe a single sou to a single soul. All the

signs were auspicious for making a fresh start.
Jerry Thompson, whom she had rung on
impulse, had received her call with whoops of
satisfaction.

'So you've finished wasting yourself on the
desert air, and about time, too! If you've nothing
else lined up, how about giving an old friend a
helping hand?'

'With pleasure. What do I do?'

'You fill in for Sandie who's been offered a
short stint with an American outfit. She's dying
to go, but I've been stalling. If you could take her
place, that'd be great. She runs a two-hour slot
late afternoon, five days a week. It's a mix of
music and interviews, snippets of topical stuff,
the odd consumer grumble, that kind of thing.'

Alyssa had grinned. 'Sounds the ideal way to
test my toes in the British radio scene again. And
who knows, if I'm working in London maybe I'll
come across a vacancy?'

'I wish I could keep you for myself, but
present economies mean I can't add to permanent
staff,' Jerry had replied. 'And suppose you take
over Sandie's flat while she's away? It's small,
but stunning. Old Sandie has a bit of a flair for
interior decorating.'

Old Sandie, it transpired, had more than a bit
of flair. One half of the upper floor of a Victorian
villa in Hampstead had been gutted to provide
avant garde living space with bijou bedroom,
bathroom and kitchen cleverly hinged on. Bright
screenprints flanked doorways and mirrors had
been utilised to suggest space. All-white walls
carried intricate paintings in stained glass colours,

there was a jazzy selection of straw hats and wicker cartwheels over the chimney breast, and on a pedestal by the window a magnificent tiger's head fashioned from gold wire and semi-precious stones snarled in silence.

Down three steps from the living area was the bedroom. Here the ceiling had been cunningly draped to reproduce the illusion of a tent, and the muted shades of buttercup and jade were repeated in the wallpaper, the padded bedhead and the frilled duvet. Waking up there was like waking up amidst a verdant landscape.

Yet spectacular though it was, there was something the flat lacked—peace. In addition to taking over Sandie's job and home, Alyssa also appeared to have taken over Sandie's friends. There was always someone knocking at the door. During her four weeks in London, she had played impromptu hostess to copywriters and water-ski enthusiasts, clinked glasses with schoolteachers and entrepreneurs. She had been talked at until three in the morning, pressed to join a kibbutz, and received umpteen invitations out. This automatic entrée to a brand new social life should have made her step springy, her smile wide—common sense told her that, as well. A Nordic gentleman who came calling had transferred his affections from Old Sandie, and if she so much as crooked a finger he would be hers to command. But she didn't want a Nordic gentleman, she wanted Tariq. So much for common sense, she thought despairingly.

Chin on her hand, Alyssa stirred her coffee. She was in the radio station canteen—her

daily programme been and gone—and in no rush
to get back to the decorator's dream. Here it was
peaceful, with just two or three weary souls
scattered amongst the tables minding their own
business. Why must she act like a love-sick
schoolgirl? she wondered with a sigh. Why waste
time and energy moping? Why couldn't she accept
that the day at the oasis had been a magic day,
but a day separate from the rest of her life? She
had known from the very start their relationship
was doomed, so why sit and pine—pine for a man
who had used her once before discarding her like
a crumpled tissue? But their lovemaking had been
pure and beautiful and incandescent, hadn't it?
Tariq had been as overwhelmed as she, hadn't
he? Alyssa offered up a soundless howl. Face
facts. Tariq had never once tried to deceive her.
He had been open about his forthcoming
marriage. Maybe he had intended for her to be
his mistress—everyone wants me for their
damned mistress, she thought savagely—but that
was all. So why persuade herself something
special had existed between them? There was no
reason to believe he loved her. Though he *had*
said, 'Alyssa Brett, I love you', so perhaps he
had, just for one day? Could love start and stop
within the space of twenty-four hours? His
maybe. Never hers.

Alyssa found herself reliving the interview with
Sheikh Suroor.

'Tariq does not want you here,' he had said.

In the cold clear light of London, it was
obvious that by banishing her Tariq had been
using his common sense. So why didn't she use

hers and admit that, uncharacteristic though it seemed, he had employed someone else to do his dirty work? His uncle had been eager to remove her from the sheikhdom for his own reasons, but Tariq must have been in full agreement. Perhaps the gardener at the oasis had rung straight through to report what he had seen, and Tariq had arrived back at the coast palace to face an almighty row? He may not have been happy to send her away, but he would have recognised his priorities. But suppose, just suppose, Sheikh Suroor had acted without his nephew's knowledge. Don't be an idiot, she chided. On his return from Oslo, Tariq must have discovered what had happened. If he had cared he would have taken steps to contact her. He would have been desperate to apologise, explain, disclaim responsibility. But he had not made contact. She had heard nothing.

No longer did she awake in the night fretting about Douglas and the troubles he had incurred, but she still woke. The day Alyssa had cleared the debt had been the day she had emotionally buried her husband. The transaction had been a point of departure when she had been able to put Douglas's role in her life into perspective. Any feelings of guilt had gone. She accepted she had done her best for him, both alive and dead. She could remember him peacefully. Yet all she had done was exchange one ghost for another—Tariq haunted her now.

Vaguely aware of a figure threading its way through the tables, she looked up when a hand rested on her shoulder.

'You never whistled, kid, but I came all the same,' a mock Humphrey Bogart said through squiffy mouth.

'Lennie! What are you doing here? Why aren't you in Ras-Al-Khan? You haven't been fired?' she demanded in a rush.

'No, I haven't been fired,' he laughed, peeling off a cream leather coat.

Wrenched from her futile ponderings to be confronted by someone who would have news of Tariq, she felt jittery.

'Why are you in London? How's Brough? Any word about—oh, about anyone?' Alyssa finished up awkwardly.

'Let me buy us both a coffee, then I'll reveal all.'

Reveal all about Tariq? she wondered, as Lennie went to the self-service counter. Did she want revelations? Could she cope with them? Wasn't knowing nothing better?

'I'm here in the U.K. for a mixture of holiday and work,' he said, returning with steaming mugs. 'In addition to visiting my folks and friends, I'm hoping to set up interviews with some of the celebrities who'll be appearing in Ras-Al-Khan's hotels over the winter. Radio exposure's advance publicity for them, plus good old-fashioned entertainment for the listeners. Also Mohammed's fixed up for me to see some guys at the BBC, plus I'm sniffing around independent stations to update myself on the latest happenings in the pop scene.'

Alyssa wrinkled her nose. 'What's gone wrong? This urge for work doesn't sound like you.'

He debated whether or not to take offence, then grinned. 'Okay, so I wasn't exactly co-operating when you rushed off. But what you see before you is the born-again Lennie Leith. A few months ago I'd got myself on a downward conveyor, and I guess Tariq slammed on a brake, made me see sense.'

'How is His Excellency?' She had more or less promised herself she wouldn't ask, but the words sneaked out.

'Fine. He made the front page of the *Ras-Al-Khan Times* the other day.'

'His—his wedding?' she croaked, feeling legless.

'No. When it was announced he's to be Minister of Petroleum and Mineral Resources. He's being formally appointed in about five weeks' time.' Lennie sipped his coffee. 'Oddly enough, Tariq's in England right now.' Alyssa froze. She longed to ask why, but was terrified of croaking again. Maybe he was over here on honeymoon? Or had he brought Shamsa to meet his mother? 'He's taking part in some Oxford seminar which is studying world energy issues,' the disc jockey continued, and she felt weak with relief.

'And how's my old friend, Brough?' she asked, almost gaily.

'Still writing plays. He's forever racking his tiny mind for meaningful phrases. Last week he——'

It took Lennie half an hour to bring her up to date, then she gave him her news, liberally larding her exploits in London with enthusiasm.

'Sounds like you've fallen on your feet,' Lennie grinned when she finished.

Alyssa gave a wide, plastic smile. 'Leaving Ras-Al-Khan was the best thing that ever happened to me.'

A couple of evenings later, she was back at the flat when there was the ominous sound of footsteps on the stairs.

'Hard luck, mate,' she hissed beneath her breath. 'I refuse to be sociable tonight.' Arms circling her knees, chin to her chest, Alyssa huddled in the corner of the sofa and shot arrows of resentment at the closed door. The steps had halted, and a finger had pressed the bell once, twice, a third time. 'For heaven's sake,' she grumbled, and hurled herself forward. She wrenched open the door. 'If you would kindly take your finger off that damn bell and——' Her mouth stayed open, but the words stopped tumbling out. She recovered quickly. 'What do you want?' she demanded.

Bulked out by a sheepskin jacket worn over brown sweater and slacks, Tariq waited on the landing. His long legs were set apart, and he looked horribly like a man with a mission.

'There are some questions I need answered.'

'Sorry, I'm not in the question answering mood,' Alyssa announced, and would have closed the door if he hadn't thrust one broad shoulder.

Shrugging off his jacket, Tariq made a slow and shrewd assessment of his surroundings. 'So this is where the twenty thousand went? I congratulate you.'

'The flat happens to be rented, and I wasn't responsible for the décor,' she snapped, his sneering arrogance making her bristle. 'And before you say anything else I'd like to point out that I was told to leave Ras-Al-Khan by your uncle, and given a legitimate payment to cover the remainder of my contract. I didn't ask for a single penny. It was offered. So the twenty thousand pounds is——'

'You grabbed with both hands,' he accused, his voice that of prosecuting counsel. 'The offer of ready cash was so intoxicating that you damn near hijacked the next plane out in order to escape with your haul before anyone had time to change their mind.' He brushed aside her protest with a flick of dark-gold fingers. 'Suroor's account of your glee was verified by his staff. To quote his secretary, you acted as if your wildest dreams had come true.'

'Well, I was . . . pleased to receive the money,' Alyssa agreed haltingly, 'but there were reasons.'

He gave a bleak laugh. 'There always are. I presume the reason you gave for leaving—about your mother being ill—was a lie?'

'Yes, but . . .' She was confused, bewildered. Tariq had burst in and started up on an interrogation, but she needed time to think.

'And you, and all those enthusiastic ideas for improving Radio Ras-Al-Khan, disappeared into thin air.' His shrug was cruelly indifferent. 'I'm usually a fair judge of character, but I confess you had me fooled.' He shifted his stance. 'Did you never bother to wonder why you were being paid off, or by whom? Or didn't you care?'

'For God's sake, of course I care!' Alyssa's throat was stiff with pain. 'But you can't condemn me for what happened. Your uncle may have dismissed me face to face, but you were the one getting rid of me. *You!*'

'Why would I get rid of the woman I wanted to marry?' he asked, his mouth a thin line beneath his black moustache.

'Marry?' she whispered. 'But you're going to marry Shamsa.'

'No. I think deep down I've always known I could never go through with it.'

'But you never mentioned anything—anything permanent between us,' she protested, feeling weak and battered.

'I told you I loved you.'

'In passing.'

Tariq frowned. 'Is that what it sounded like? Maybe you're right. Strange as it may seem, I'd never told a woman before that I loved her.'

Alyssa's world seemed to be falling apart. 'But why didn't you say you wanted to marry me?' she implored.

'I started to. I said I'd make arrangements and explained how we needed to go carefully in order to avoid causing offence, but then you shut me up. You were tired, so was I. I was content to leave discussing the details until we were alone again.'

'But I thought you intended to install me as your mistress!'

A nerve jumped in his temple. 'As my wife. It's all hypothetical now, but I needed time to introduce the idea to my grandfather and Karim.

I also knew Suroor was bound to throw a fit when I rejected one of his daughters for the fourth time.' Tariq gave a sharp laugh. 'He did!'

'But surely your grandfather wouldn't have agreed to you marrying me?' Alyssa wailed.

'Why not? Basically all he wants is my happiness, allied to my future being committed to Ras-Al-Khan. Once he'd been assured you didn't threaten that, he would have welcomed you.'

'But——'

Tariq shrugged. 'Whether you choose to believe me or not is your prerogative.' He turned, assessing the smart décor again and closing the door on talk of marriage. 'As you didn't sink your windfall into this place, would it be impudent to ask what you plan to do with it?'

She attempted a recovery. 'The money's already spent. There was a long-standing debt to clear.'

'For twenty thousand pounds?' he drawled.

'Originally it was fifty thousand,' she said, and heard herself sound like a boasting Texan.

'How does a girl like you manage to get into debt to the tune of fifty thousand pounds?' he enquired, eyes and voice sharp. He bent to grab hold of her shoulders. 'Explain,' he commanded.

The tension of the hard fingers hinted at the control Tariq needed to summon. His face was a grim mask, yet he still wanted her, the dark lynx eyes gave that away. He wanted her, needed to touch her, yet despised her.

'I'm not prepared to go into detail,' she replied, meeting his gaze. 'But you can rest assured that the money was well spent.'

'On what?' he demanded, giving her a little shake.

'Freedom.'

'Freedom?' His laugh was ugly. 'You might have your freedom, but what about mine?' He moved one hand from her shoulder to her hip, drawing her closer towards his groin. 'What freedom do I have if I'm aroused by the mere thought of you? Rest assured you say, but how can I rest when all I do is curse you because you showed me heaven one day, and curse you because now I'm in hell?' He scoured the bristles of his moustache across her brow in a tortured motion. 'Freedom—ha! Rest—ha!'

When his mouth covered hers, it was hard and bruising. Tariq was intent on making her pay, punishing her for his unhappiness. She struggled to escape, but he refused to release her. He was forcing back her head, kissing her harder and deeper until, abruptly, the brutality of his kiss slackened. Tariq groaned something in Arabic, then his hand cradled her breast and the pressure of his mouth softened into seduction. He was pulling off her sweater, undressing her with an urgency which would have left little time for protest, even if a helpless languor had not blossomed.

'I'm the fool who loves you,' he growled, lying beside her on the bed, his dark gold hands stroking until she was on fire. 'I'm the fool who sighs over your glorious breasts, who dreams about the silken secrets of your thighs. I'm the fool who would walk round the earth just to kiss you.' He moved until he rose naked, poised above her. 'But most of all, I'm the fool who wants to spend the rest of his life doing *this* to you!'

CHAPTER ELEVEN

NEXT morning the hollow in the bed beside her was cold. When the tears stopped, Alyssa vowed she would never see Tariq again. Over the days which followed, each time she returned to the flat she felt a rush of fear and traitorous longing. Would a tall, dark figure be waiting for her? But he did not pay a second visit, and in time she accepted that their night together had provided all the answers he had needed, and cured his malaise of loving-hating her.

Yet, try as she might, she could not keep from speculating how different things might have been if only ... What would being married to Tariq have entailed? Lots of love and laughter, and the deep warm glow from knowing they belonged to each other. The public faces they would have showed to Ras-Al-Khan would have needed to be decorous, as befitted a sheikh and his wife, but in private—in private anything would have been possible. She would have cut down her radio work in order to devote a satisfactory amount of time to Tariq, but would have continued with her career until the children came along. Children—Tariq's children!

Before their marriage she and Doug had spoken about the babies they had hoped to have, but afterwards he had done an abrupt *volte face*. Now she didn't believe he had ever intended they start a family. It made sense. She could never have coped successfully with a child when she had already got Douglas who, with his moods, could change from querulous infant to repentant chum at the speed of light.

But Tariq was not Douglas. His love would not have been selfish, the greedy demanding love of an egotist. Tariq was mature, generous of spirit. He would have loved her as a partner and shared everything. There would have been no secrets, no lies, no evasions. How wonderfully restoring it would have been to be loved like that. All comfort. All sharing. All mutual respect. But he didn't love her. He didn't respect her. Not now.

Alyssa made an effort to stop yearning. At first if an hour passed by without her thinking of Tariq, she congratulated herself. Once she survived a whole morning, and wanted to wave a placard informing everyone how well she was recovering. But Lennie's 'phone call had her ripping that placard to pieces.

'Are you still here?' she mock-grumbled when Cary Grant, or was it Tony Curtis pretending to be Cary Grant? asked her out to dinner.

'Final throes. Saturday'll be a last splash before I disappear into the sandy horizon. Do say you'll join me.'

'I will. Saturday's a break off point for me, too,' she said, explaining how her stint with Jerry's radio station was over and how she was scheduled to move out of Sandie's flat.

'What happens after that?'

'I'm moving into a guest house until I can find

fresh digs. But as far as my career's concerned, that's in a state of flux.'

'Then just in case it turns out to be your last square meal before poverty threatens, how about us dining at Maxim's? Bring along your passport.'

'The Paris Maxim's?' Alyssa gasped, in surprise. 'Be serious, Lennie. Have you any idea how much a night out like that would cost?'

A chuckle rolled down the telephone wire. 'Don't pop your cork. A car'll pick you up at six tomorrow evening and deliver you to Heathrow. I'll meet you there, sweetie. Okay?'

'No, it's not okay,' she started to protest, but he cleared the line.

Maxim's? Alyssa was sure Lennie would collect her in a taxi and take her to some backstreet joint in Soho or somewhere, which had borrowed Maxim's name. That would be typical of his oddball humour.

The bronze low-cut silk jersey dress she chose to wear had been designed for evenings gazing dreamily at a man on the other side of the table, and though Lennie was the last person she'd gaze at dreamily, it seemed right for the occasion. Alyssa needed to be alluring. Tonight she wanted heads to turn, waiters to fawn, men to make eyes at her. Tariq might abuse and use, but every other male would go 'Aaahh', and need to hold on to a lamppost for support when she floated by on a drift of perfume.

Eyelids stroked with bronze, mascara thickly applied, Alyssa twisted her freshly shampooed

hair into an ashen loop and secured it with gold
pins. Gold stud earrings were being screwed into
place when the blast of a car horn drew her to the
window. It was precisely six o'clock, and a black
Mercedes was parked at the kerb. Her conviction
that Maxim's was a non-starter took a battering.
She slipped on a velvet evening jacket, grabbed
her purse, and ran downstairs.

'Could you collecting me be some kind of a
joke?' she asked the driver, as they sped along the
motorway. The airport was drawing closer by the
minute, and still she found it difficult to accept
Lennie really intended for them to dine at the
Paris Maxim's.

'Don't ask me, love,' he smiled. 'The car hire
was fixed over the 'phone, that's all I know.'

To her bewilderment, when they reached
Heathrow the driver passed by the three terminals
and headed instead for a much quieter area. He
braked before the entrance to an unmarked, low
brick building, and turned.

'Here we are. Go through the swing doors and
take the corridor to your left. The instructions
said the gentleman would be waiting in the third
room on the right.'

Feeling very much like Alice in Wonderland—
curiouser and curiouser—Alyssa set off down the
corridor. Reaching the third door on the right,
she halted and knocked.

'*Ta'ala*,' a familiar voice commanded.

For a moment she was incredulous, then,
'No,' she muttered to herself. '*No!*' she said out
loud.

Refusing to be ensnared, she whirled and sped

back along the corridor as fast as she could go. Behind her, the door opened.

'Alyssa, wait!'

The sound of footsteps behind warned Tariq was rapidly drawing level.

'Leave me alone,' she spat, batting blindly with an arm to keep him away, but he gripped her shoulder and dragged her to a halt. She glared up into his lynx eyes. 'Leave me alone!'

Her voice was verging on shrillness, but she didn't care. She didn't care either when an amused voice said, 'Excuse us,' and a couple of air stewardesses walked past. Her flushed and irate face proved cause for comment as well as giggles, and the girls kept looking back over their shoulders.

'Come into the lounge where we can talk,' Tariq coaxed.

'No way!'

'Alyssa, I pack a darn sight more muscle power than you,' he warned.

'What do you intend to do—drag me in by the hair, or use chloroform?' she taunted.

'Just this.' He whisked her up into his arms and marched along the corridor. Back in the lounge, he tumbled her down on to a white leather sofa with no ceremony at all. 'Forgive the he-man stuff, but you only have yourself to blame,' he said, grinning down to where she made a pink-faced bundle.

Alyssa struggled to her feet and gathered up as much dignity as she could muster. 'No, *you're* to blame. Why have you brought me here? I'm not prepared to be your——' her voice cracked, 'your slave girl. I'm not at your beck and call.'

'Indeed, you're not. You've made that perfectly plain. But attempting to speak to you at the flat would have been a waste of time. You'd have slammed the door in my face.'

'I wouldn't have even *opened* it.'

'That's what I thought. That's why it seemed preferable to get you on to my territory.'

Blue eyes still blazing, Alyssa took a hasty note of their surroundings. The room was far more luxurious than airport lounges she had visited in the past; the deep-pile carpet was embossed gold and the sofas were of fine-grained leather. Newspapers and the latest magazines were spread on low teak tables, and for those who required something meatier, one wall was lined with shelves which carried a wealth of leather-bound books.

'And how is this your territory?' she demanded.

'Not exactly mine. A handful of other businessmen do use the lounge, though we shan't be disturbed this evening. Suroor, with his flair for wasting money, fixed a deal whereby he has a part-share in the place. However, I'm negotiating with the authorities for some other spendthrift to take it over.'

Alyssa raised a disdainful brow. 'Your uncle became bored with being part-owner of an airport lounge?'

'My uncle became dead.'

'Dead?' she echoed. 'When did he die?'

'The day after you and I last met,' Tariq said,

walking over to a small bar in the corner of the room. He fixed a couple of drinks and came back, handing her a glass filled with what proved to be martini on the rocks. 'He'd been ill for quite a while, but the end was sudden. My grandfather called me back to Ras-Al-Khan, and I had no alternative but to go. There was the funeral to attend, and obviously the death of the heir meant rearrangement of a wide variety of matters, both governmental and private. I'm afraid this is the first opportunity I've had to get in touch.'

'As far as I'm concerned, there was no need for you to bother getting in touch,' Alyssa replied acidly. 'No contact has suited me just fine.' She set the barely touched drink down on a side table. 'I'm going now, but before I leave I'd be grateful if you'd explain one thing.'

'What's that?'

'How you managed to coerce Lennie into siding against me? Devious he is but I was under the illusion he had a soft spot for me. I thought he was my friend!'

Tariq regarded her with something suspiciously like amusement.

'Lennie believes that I'm taking you out to dinner because you were a valued member of Radio Ras-Al-Khan's broadcasting team. I explained I wanted to thank you for your work, but didn't have chance earlier, due to your swift departure.'

'Top marks for ingenuity!' Alyssa was cryptic. 'But why does he imagine I left in the first place? And didn't he think Maxim's a trifle over the top for a boss and employee thank you?'

'Lennie tends to believe anything of oil sheikhs.' Now it was Tariq's turn to be cryptic. 'I hinted that homesickness had been responsible for your departure, and he accepted it.'

'Lennie might be prepared to accept what you say, do what you want, but——' Suddenly she stopped. Further words refused to come for he had leant forward and taken hold of her hand. Bringing it to his lips, he was involved in kissing her fingertips, one by one. The look in his eyes was making her skin prickle. 'Please don't,' Alyssa implored, though her protest was weak and she could not take her hand from his grasp. 'Please don't make me——'

'Make you do what, *habibati*?' He opened his mouth and gently sucked at a forefinger, his dark eyes watching her reaction.

'Make me want you all over again.'

'But I'm not making you do anything,' Tariq murmured.

'You are! You're making me want you, making me need you. Making me feel as though my life and my happiness depend on you,' she wailed.

'Cliff reckons it's time you had someone to depend on, instead of people always depending on you.'

Her eyes widened. 'You've spoken to Cliff?'

He nodded. 'I've spoken to him and Meg and I paid a visit to an unpleasant individual called Dutton.'

'When?' she demanded, snatching her hand away.

'Two days ago, the moment I was free of Ras-Al-Khan.' His look was sombre. 'I still needed answers. Too many things didn't make sense. Why didn't you tell me about the trouble you were in?' he asked roughly. 'I'd have understood. I would have cleared the debt straight away.'

Alyssa stared at her shoes. 'I couldn't. I couldn't take your money.'

His smile was tender. 'That's your weakness, *habibati*. You never take, do you? You always give.'

'Did—did Meg and Cliff say much about Doug?' she enquired haltingly.

'They told me what they could, but Cliff said he'd never understood your attitude. You're a cool-headed, intelligent woman, so why didn't you bring your influence to bear on your husband? Why didn't you calm him down, keep him out of debt?'

'I couldn't.' It was a whisper.

'Why not?' When she remained silent, Tariq tried another tack. 'Alyssa, it'd be wrong for us to start our married life with Douglas casting a long shadow.'

'Married life?' A sudden contraction of her lungs left her breathless.

He reached for her hand again, kissing the exposed palm. 'I love you and I'm sure you love me, so isn't marriage the proper sequence of events? I suppose we could always live in sin,' he teased, when she just looked at him. 'But if we try that in Ras-Al-Khan, there's the danger we'll be hauled before the courts and stoned in punishment.'

She grinned. 'That's out. I bruise easily.'

'In which case, will you marry me?'

'Yes, please!'

Tariq took her in his arms and began kissing her as though his life depended on it.

'We're being diverted,' he said, when eventually they managed to break apart. 'I want to know about your life with Douglas.' He sensed her slight withdrawal. 'All about it, *habibati*.'

Now Alyssa withdrew physically, moving from the circle of his arms to sit a little way from him on the sofa. Her spine was stiff, her face set. She took a deep breath and began to speak. Hesitantly at first, her tale gathered momentum until it was as if a dam had been ruptured and the words were flooding out. Halfway through, she sighed.

'I never knew matters were as bad as they turned out to be. I'd guessed Doug might well leave some bills which needed to be settled, but I'd imagined they'd be minor ones. I had some money set aside for a rainy day, so I thought I'd use that and pay off any debts without too much trouble.'

'You realise Cliff had suspicions about Douglas's viability all along?'

There was a half smile. 'Oh yes. Cliff has always been alert to the nuances. So many times I've been on the brink of explaining—since Doug's death, I mean—but that would've involved admitting Doug had married me under false pretences, so to speak, and that he'd lied about his business affairs.' Alyssa swallowed hard. 'Cliff never did rate him very highly, and if I'd told the truth he'd have thought even less of him. I didn't want that.'

'So you protected him—alive and dead.'

Tariq held her close and listened intently as more revelations spilled out. When her tale was ended, he kissed her, murmuring soothing words, calming her, telling her that now she was with him and safe, but a knock at the door and a discreet cough broke them apart.

A steward came in. From the brief Arabic exchange, Alyssa picked out 'Ras-Al-Khan' and '*tayara*' which she knew meant plane.

'You're not returning to the Gulf tonight, are you?' she wailed, when the steward had disappeared.

He nodded. 'I'm afraid there's no Maxim's. Never was. That was embroidery for Lennie's sake.'

'But you can't leave me now,' she protested.

'Who said anything about leaving you? You have brought your passport?' She nodded dumbly. 'Can I have it? Just for the formalities.'

'What formalities?' Alyssa gave her head a little shake, trying to clear her senses. 'You don't expect me to fly with you to Ras-Al-Khan right now, on the spur of the moment?'

'Why not?' He held out his hand. 'Come along, the plane's waiting.'

'But——' She continued to protest as he led her out into the corridor, across the tarmac and towards a black, white and gold jet, painted with the Al Zahini family crest. 'But how long will we be away?' she asked, climbing the metal steps.

There was a pause as the steward welcomed them aboard. Tariq gave instructions about a meal which was to be served later, and drinks which were to be served immediately, and then took her elbow and steered her into the main cabin.

'We'll return to London in a week's time,' he said, when they were sitting in armchairs sipping fresh martinis. 'Five days from now my appointment as Minister of Petroleum is to be ratified and, very selfishly, I want you to share that with me. My mother's to fly out, also. Hatchets have been buried at long last,' he explained, when he saw her look of surprise. 'My uncle was the one who kept the feud alive, and now that he's gone everything is easier. Sheikh Ahmad, my grandfather, issued an invitation to my mother himself.' Tariq grinned. 'Incidentally, I'd better warn you that my mother has a house on her land which has been earmarked for years as an English base for me and my wife, so be prepared for the hard sell. But don't commit yourself to anything. We'll go and have a look at it on our return, and make up our own minds.'

Alyssa gave him a teasing glance. 'You're frightened your mother might talk me into something?'

'No, I think you have a mind of your own.' He smiled, squeezing her fingers as the jet engines began to hum, ready for take-off. 'But mothers-in-law are mothers-in-law.'

'Wait until you meet yours,' she giggled, then sobered. On reflection, it was probable her mother could turn out to be Tariq's arch-fan. She looked around the elegant coffee-and-cream cabin. 'I didn't know you had your own plane.'

'Come on,' he protested. 'You know me

better than that.'

'Not Suroor again?'

'Another of his follies,' Tariq confirmed. 'But enjoy it while you can because I've located a Texas oil baron who's willing to take it over. The plane's being returned to Ras-Al-Khan where it'll be stripped of my uncle's embellishments, then it'll be fitted out as a flying office before it's delivered to the States. Come and have a look round.'

The jet was amazing.

'Even better than dining at Maxim's,' Alyssa declared, as she was shown the galley where the steward displayed hot plates and fridges, and allowed her a sniff at the duck *à l'orange* which was being prepared. The pilot was especially proud of his compartment, and during their five minutes on the flightdeck gave a glowing account of the aircraft's technical splendour. A cabin which seemed part cinema, part computer centre came next, followed by a bathroom with fur carpet and jacuzzi. Back into the elegant coffee-and-cream cabin, then through to what Tariq sardonically called the 'fun room', which had pinball machines and a vast stereo.

'What, no billiard table?' Alyssa asked, in mock horror.

'Even Suroor had his limits,' he grinned, shaking a doleful head. He led her into the final cabin, a bedroom. Here walls were covered in a deep rose silk, the carpet was a lush white pile, and the bed . . .

'If you ask why my uncle needed a four-poster, I'll have to pass,' he smiled, seeing her amazement. 'It needed to be built *in situ*, which means that very shortly it's to be dismantled.'

'What a shame.' Alyssa touched the white satin-and-lace coverlet, marvelled at the white gauzy curtains. 'It's a beautiful bed.'

He slid his arm around her waist and pulled her against him. 'Have you ever made love in a four-poster?' he murmured, nibbling at her ear.

She nestled closer. 'No.'

'Have you ever made love at thirty-five thousand feet?'

'No.'

'Like to try both?' Tariq enquired, kissing a particularly vulnerable spot on her throat.

'What about the steward?'

'If he wants to try, he must find his own partner,' he said vaguely, finding a sudden interest in the neckline of her dress where the honeyed swell of her breasts needed to be kissed.

'But suppose the steward comes in?' she protested, pushing back and making him look at her.

'The door has locks, the duck *à l'orange* will wait. My steward will only interrupt if the plane's about to crash.'

'That's very decent of him.'

'All my staff are well trained,' Tariq grinned. 'Only my wife needs subduing, as I seem to remember telling you before.' He pointed imperiously towards the bed. '*Imshi!*' he commanded.

Alyssa began to smile. 'Yes, master,' she said. 'Oh, yes.'

ROMANCE

Rebecca had set herself on course for loneliness and despair. It took a plane crash and a struggle to survive in the wilds of the Canadian Northwest Territories to make her change – and to let her fall in love with the only other survivor, handsome Guy McLaren.

Arctic Rose is her story – and you can read it from the 14th February for just £2.25.

The story continues with Rebecca's sister, Tamara, available soon.

Take 4
Exciting Books
Absolutely
FREE

Love, romance, intrigue... all are captured for you by Mills & Boon's top-selling authors. By becoming a regular reader of Mills & Boon's Romances you can enjoy 6 superb new titles every month plus a whole range of special benefits: your very own personal membership card, a free monthly newsletter packed with recipes, competitions, exclusive book offers and a monthly guide to the stars, plus extra bargain offers and big cash savings.

**AND an Introductory FREE GIFT for YOU.
Turn over the page for details.**

As a special introduction we will send you four exciting Mills & Boon Romances Free and without obligation when you complete and return this coupon.

At the same time we will reserve a subscription to Mills & Boon Reader Service for you. Every month, you will receive 6 of the very latest novels by leading Romantic Fiction authors, delivered direct to your door. You don't pay extra for delivery — postage and packing is always completely Free. There is no obligation or commitment — you can cancel your subscription at any time.

You have nothing to lose and a whole world of romance to gain.

Just fill in and post the coupon today to **MILLS & BOON READER SERVICE, FREEPOST, P.O. BOX 236, CROYDON, SURREY CR9 9EL.**

Please Note:- READERS IN SOUTH AFRICA write to Mills & Boon, Postbag X3010, Randburg 2125, S. Africa.

FREE BOOKS CERTIFICATE

To: Mills & Boon Reader Service, FREEPOST, P.O. Box 236, Croydon, Surrey CR9 9EL.

Please send me, free and without obligation, four Mills & Boon Romances, and reserve a Reader Service Subscription for me. If I decide to subscribe I shall, from the beginning of the month following my free parcel of books, receive six new books each month for £6.60, post and packing free. If I decide not to subscribe, I shall write to you within 10 days. The free books are mine to keep in any case. I understand that I may cancel my subscription at any time simply by writing to you. I am over 18 years of age.

Please write in BLOCK CAPITALS.

Signature _____

Name _____

Address _____

_____ Post code _____

SEND NO MONEY — TAKE NO RISKS.

Please don't forget to include your Postcode.

Remember, postcodes speed delivery. Offer applies in UK only and is not valid to present subscribers. Mills & Boon reserve the right to exercise discretion in granting membership. If price changes are necessary you will be notified.

6R Offer expires 31st March 1986.

EP86